FROM MANHATTAN
WITH REVENGE

FROM MANHATTAN WITH REVENGE

BY CHRISTOPHER SMITH

ACKNOWLEDGMENTS

For their help with this book, the author is particularly grateful to Erich Kaiser, his parents Ross Smith and Ann Smith, Margaret Nagle, Kate Cady, J. Carson Black, Laura Baumgardner, Ellen Beck, Jackie Kennedy, Angel Davis, Anna Dobson, Tyler Thiede, the team at Odyl, his friends at the Bangor Daily News and at UMaine, Sandy Phippen, Debra McCann, Diane Cormier, Lisa Smith, Deborah Rogers, Howard Segal, Brandi Doane, and his amazing accountant and financial advisor, Jaime Berube. To all of you, I appreciate it.

The author also would like to thank his readers, who are the lifeblood of his work. Thank you for your patience and your support. You are the first and last reason for every early morning and late night. I'll see you on Facebook.

Additional thanks to the Amazon team; his friends Ted Adams and Bari Khan for exposing him to the darker side of Manhattan, even if they didn't know they were doing so at the time; to those other unnamed men and women who introduced the author to the real Manhattan while he researched this book; and to friends, old and new, all of whom either helped to shape this book or who offered support as it was written.

Thank you.

Books by
Christopher Smith

In the United States

Fifth Avenue Series
Fifth Avenue: Book One
Running of the Bulls: Book Two
From Manhattan with Love: Novella Three
The *Fifth Avenue* Series (Box Set)
A Rush to Violence
From Manhattan with Revenge
From Manhattan with Love and Revenge (Box Set)

Bullied Series
Bullied: Book One
Revenge: Book Two
Witch: Book Three
War: Book Four
The Complete Bullied Series

Stand-Alone Books
You Only Die Twice

BOOK ONE

CHAPTER ONE

She was being followed. She was aware of it. And she was prepared to act when they acted.

If they have a chance.

It was nighttime in Manhattan. Past eleven. Earlier, she tried to sleep, but since sleep no longer came as easily as it used to, she was walking down Fifth, because outside, the city offered distractions she needed to lean on right now.

The Park was next to her. The cool fall breeze carried with it the smells of the city—exhaust from the cabs darting past her to her left, the rot of damp foliage off to her right, but also a crispness that hadn't been in the mix when she was here three weeks ago.

Winter was coming. It was right at her back, not unlike the sound of those shoes keeping time with hers as she strolled down the sidewalk.

Carmen Gragera listened to those shoes. She first became aware of them when she turned onto Fifth from Eighty-First Street, where she kept an apartment. At some point, she knew they'd find her, especially since she was back in the city.

What they didn't know is that she also had come back for them.

She had returned to Manhattan three days ago, after burying her fellow assassin and lover, Alex Williams, in Bora Bora, where he was murdered while they were on vacation. There, they had been making plans to leave their professional lives as assassins behind so they could be together in a tropical paradise that offered a measure of security due to the sheer remoteness the island provided.

But with his murder and the burning down of her longtime home, it proved a costly assumption. For reasons that still were unclear to her, the syndicate she and Alex worked for killed Alex and tried to kill her. She managed to escape, but now they were after her.

After all, the sound of those shoes didn't lie.

She could tell by the definitive strike of the footfalls that they belonged to a man. When would he act? She didn't know, but in her coat pocket was her Glock; her hand was wrapped around it and she'd use it if necessary.

Unless he shot her in the back, which was possible, though it would be stupid on his part given that they were on Fifth, which was alive with traffic.

She could feel him behind her. The footsteps were coming closer. She kept her pace steady, her body loose. Fifty feet. Forty. Closing the gap and doing so in such a way that was so obvious, it was amateurish. Why was he giving himself away like this?

He was probably twenty feet away from her when she approached Seventy-Seventh Street. The traffic light was red and there was a line of cabs waiting for the light to change. Grab one? Plenty were empty. But if the light didn't change quickly, he might be brazen enough to approach the cab and shoot her, because otherwise, he would have missed his chance and disappointed whoever hired him.

Best to move on.

She looked as far down the sidewalk as she could and saw others coming toward her. The area was well lit, just bright enough to quell a murder, unless the man following her was determined to take her out.

Again possible, but again, stupid. Still, who knew what his orders were? Who knew if he was just young and naive enough to believe he could pull this off? If he was, she was ready for it.

In fact, when the light turned green and traffic roared to life, she decided she'd had enough. She stopped and faced him.

He also stopped. Their eyes met. He wasn't the young man she was expecting. Instead, he looked somewhere in his late thirties. Tall. Brown hair. Good looking. Wearing a knee-length black coat to keep out the cold and also to better conceal whatever he was carrying.

"Carmen Gragera?" he asked.

She watched his hands. Said nothing. A couple brushed past them, the woman's head on the man's shoulder. Carmen could smell the flowery perfume the woman left in her wake.

"You and I should talk," he said. "I'm a friend of Alex Williams."

"That's your first mistake," she said. "Alex didn't have any friends."

His brow furrowed. "What gives you that idea?"

"Maybe you meant to say you were colleagues?"

"That's not what I meant to say. I was his friend. Since childhood."

"Then you know Alex well. Where did he grow up?"

"Indianapolis."

Anyone could know that, but only those closest to Alex would know what she was about to ask. During their last two weeks together, when they spoke freely about their private lives, he brought up the one topic that haunted him most. It was something he said he'd never be able to live down. Not with himself, not with his family.

"What was Alex's biggest regret?"

"There were a few things."

"Why not take a shot at one of them?"

"Should I start with his family?"

"If you want."

"OK, so you want the obvious one. Alex regretted not being there for his father's death. He had the opportunity to catch a flight and spend some time with him, but instead he chose to take another job. He thought his father had more time. He was wrong. He died while Alex was away. Alex regretted that, and when he asked me if I agreed that he'd made a mistake, I told him that he had. He knew better. He should have been there."

It was the correct answer. He took a step closer and she took a step back. *Watch his hands.*

"I'm not here to hurt you."

"Even if you were, I'd kill you first."

"I'm here to help you."

"Help me with what?"

"I work for Katzev." He raised his eyebrows as if in bemusement. "Strike that. I used to work for Katzev. Now, he wants me dead just like he wants you dead. If we talk frankly, we might be able to help each other. I think that would be a smart idea."

"How do I know you're not working for him now?"

"You don't."

"Well, there's a balm of reassurance. Take your hands out of your pockets."

He did.

"Who are you?"

He looked around him. "We should get a cab," he said. "I'll tell you what you want to know inside. Right now, we're too exposed."

"Can't handle it?"

"After what happened last night, I'll admit I'm on edge."

"What happened last night?"

"They came after me. I'm lucky to be alive."

"I wonder how lucky that makes me."

He didn't answer.

"How did you find me?"

"Do you want the 101 version, Carmen? I used my contacts. You were seen at LaGuardia. You were followed to your apartment on Fifth and Eighty-First. Done."

"Bullshit. I wasn't followed."

"Sorry, but you were."

"Nobody followed me. I would have known."

"Apparently, you didn't, because you were followed, just as you and Alex were followed to Bora Bora." He paused. "Which you also knew about. Right?"

Obviously, she didn't know. Point taken.

"I received a call from Alex not long before his death. It was just before you went to the island. He told me he was in love with you, which concerned me. You have a reputation for being arrogant. I told him to stay away from you."

"I wish he had. He'd be alive now."

"We don't know that. All we know is that Alex and you were targeted, and now I am too. Why?"

"I don't know."

"Then maybe we should help each other figure it out before we both wind up dead."

"What's your name?"

He didn't answer.

She sighed. "Then, what do you want me to call you?"

"Jake."

"Jake?"

"You got something better?"

"I'm Carmen Gragera," she said. "But you already know that. We'll call you Jake for now. When you're comfortable telling me the truth and that your name is probably Hamlisch, or worse, we'll likely be on better terms. As for now, you're Jake." She nodded at the street. "So, Jake, let's grab that cab so you can tell me everything you think I need to know. I'm eager to hear."

CHAPTER TWO

In the cab, they told the driver they were new to the city and that they just wanted to drive around and enjoy the night. The driver, a middle-aged woman with dark hair pulled back in a thick braid, was happy to oblige.

"I'll give you the full show," she said.

"Perfect," Carmen said. "Would you mind a bit of music?"

"What type?"

"Dance?"

"You got it."

"Thanks."

The driver turned up the volume and they drove down Fifth. The thump, thump, thump of the driving dance beat was just loud enough to conceal their voices. It would be awhile before she trusted this Jake person, but his hands had yet to dip back into his pockets and he was correct about Alex's chief regret. Her hand was still around her gun. She was ready to act if she thought for a moment that he was a shill. Still, she had to give him a chance, because if he was legit, he might have information she could use.

"How long have you worked for the syndicate?" she asked, keeping her voice low.

"Three years."

"How many jobs?"

"A dozen? Fifteen?"

"You don't know exactly?"

"I work for a few different organizations."

"Who doesn't? Over the past seven years, I've done twenty-two jobs for them. So, I'll ask again. How many?"

He thought for a moment. "After last week, fourteen."

"Who was last week?"

"There were two. Each a board member at Light Corp."

"How'd you do it?"

"I was told by Katzev to shoot each in the head."

As far as Carmen was concerned, before his death, Jean-Georges Laurent was the former unofficial head of a syndicate she knew very little about, which is how they wanted it. He tried to trick her and Alex into killing each other, but it didn't work. They found out about it, which was bad luck for Laurent, who was tracked down and took their bullets in his face instead.

"Have you ever met Katzev?"

"Never. You?"

She shook her head. While Laurent had been her chief contact at the syndicate, she often worked directly with the person she assumed was second in charge—Katzev. With Laurent dead, Carmen had to assume that Katzev now was leading the syndicate. "We've only spoken via encrypted e-mails and satellite cell phones, each untraceable. And I doubt his name is Katzev."

"Maybe it's Hamlisch."

Carmen ignored the joke. She didn't know this man and she certainly didn't know if she could trust him. She was willing to listen to what he had to say, but not without her gun trained on him. "What happened last night?"

"Two men came after me."

"Details?"

"I was having dinner under the Gowanus in Brooklyn. I've gone to the same restaurant for years. It's a hole in the wall, but I like it there because the food is OK, it sits on a corner, and it's obscure. It blends in on a street filled with porn shops and similar low-rent joints."

"Sounds perfect."

"For people like us, it is."

"I was being serious."

"The layout is good," he said. "You can sit at the rear of the restaurant, facing the front glass door while keeping an eye on it. I was keeping my eye on it. Two men walked past the door twice during the hour I was sitting there. I recognized one of them. I did a job with him once for Katzev. I knew what happened to you and to Alex, so I saw what was coming. I ordered another coffee and waited for night to fall. When it was dark, I approached one of the owners. He knows me as a regular. I asked if there was another way out. Without missing a beat, he took me to a side door. No questions asked. The door led to a side street. With the exception of some transients, it's kind of dead down there, which is another reason I like it. When I stepped outside, the man I didn't recognize was on the sidewalk having a cigarette. He was startled to see me, but before he could drop the cigarette and reach for his gun, I had my arms around him and crushed his chest. It was quick. I lowered him to the pavement so he was leaning against a car. He didn't look dead so much as he looked passed out. The owner watched all of it. When I finished, I looked over at him and he just sort of shrugged and said, 'Coffee?' I declined."

"What about the other man?"

"He was the challenge."

"How so?"

"He came after me. He was younger. Faster. In fact, he was really fast. We ran several blocks before I took a chance and ran into oncoming traffic. I was lucky and made it to the other side. He was unlucky and got flattened by a truck. End of story, at least for last night. More is coming. Not just for me, but for both of us."

"You know I'll be able to verify his death."

"I expect you to. We need to get on the same page, Carmen. I need you to trust me before they reach us. Or I can just leave. We can tackle this individually. It's up to you. But there's something to be said for joining forces and finding out why this is happening. Why do they want us dead? Why did they kill Alex? We must know something they don't want us to know. Do you have any idea what that could be?"

"I've been racking my brain since they attacked us. I have nothing."

"Do you have any way to reach Katzev?"

"Encrypted e-mails. Satellite cell phones."

"Same here."

"We wait for them," Carmen said. "But that doesn't mean I can't find out more about him, maybe even where he lives. No one is completely safe or invisible. We both know that."

She checked her watch, saw that it was approaching midnight, and had an idea. She leaned toward the driver and raised her voice above the music. "That was great," she said. "The city is beautiful. Would you drop us at the Waldorf?"

"Sounds romantic."

"I hear they have a great bar," Carmen said.

CHAPTER THREE

When they arrived at the Waldorf Astoria's Peacock Alley Bar, each ordered a martini and a glass of water, though they'd only touch the water. They bought the drink to satisfy the bartender.

"They won't think to look for us here," she said. "Let me make a phone call. Give me a few minutes and I'll be back."

She maneuvered her way out of the bar, took a right, walked down a corridor lined with Art Deco brass elevators on one side and restrooms on the other before she entered the massive lobby.

It was a Thursday night and it was late. The few chairs along the periphery were empty. She chose one just beneath the grand piano, which was elevated above her on the mezzanine, and sat down.

There was only one person she knew who might be able to help her through this—her colleague Vincent Spocatti. He was the best in the business. He had more skills, instincts, and contacts than anyone she knew. After working with him a year ago on a Wall Street job, she hoped he wouldn't mind a call from her now.

She found his number on her cell and dialed.

If anyone knew anything about Katzev, how she could get close to him or find out where he lived, it was Spocatti. And if he didn't know, he probably knew someone who would.

"Carmen," he said when he answered. "Surprised to hear from you. What am I to read into that?"

"That I'm in trouble."

"I heard about Alex," he said. "Sorry. I liked him. I also hear that you liked him."

She didn't reply.

"Where are you now?"

"At a hotel in Manhattan. You?"

"Behind some curtains at a house in Capri."

"I see."

"What you should see are the views. Stunning."

"If this isn't a good time, Vincent—"

"The owner will be here soon, but we're fine for now. They said he might run late. What do you need?"

"I need you to help me find someone. If I've worked for him, you certainly have."

"Who is it?"

"Katzev."

"The fake Russian?"

"Katzev isn't Russian?"

"Scottish. He's got the accent down, though. I'll give him that, even if he is a bastard. Same goes for his former associate, Jean-Georges Laurent, who I hear is dead now. Bullets to the face at the Four Seasons in a room filled with people that included the likes of my old friend, Leana Redman." He let a beat pass. "Firing a gun into that crowd must have been quite a sight."

"It was."

"Nice job on that, by the way."

"I didn't do it alone."

"So, I hear."

"You hear a lot."

"I think I'm becoming something of a guru," he said. "People tell me things. That was just one conversation out of many that day. I can't remember who told me, so there's no use in asking."

She knew better. But she appreciated his discretion even if it meant she wouldn't learn who told him and why.

"So, what's going on?" he said. "How are you in trouble?"

She told him.

The syndicate she and Alex worked for targeted them for death. She wasn't sure why, but Jean-Georges Laurent nearly tricked her and Alex into killing each other. Did Laurent do it because he felt she and Alex knew too much about the organization? Impossible. She only knew what he and Katzev told her, which was minimal.

In an effort to send a message that threatening them wasn't an option, they retaliated by killing Laurent. Then, weeks later, Alex was murdered and she barely escaped death.

Now she was back in Manhattan to seek her revenge.

"The people who killed Alex," Spocatti said. "Why are you convinced it had anything to do with the syndicate?"

"Because we killed Laurent."

"So? You and Alex have taken down dozens of people over the course of your careers. It could have been anyone. Why them?"

"Because for whatever reason, Laurent wanted us dead. I'm sure there are others who'd like to see that happen, but I'm not directly aware of them."

"Just because you're not aware of them doesn't mean someone else isn't targeting you."

"Do you know something I don't?"

"I usually do," Spocatti said. "But not this time. Just keep your options open. Anyone could have it in for you. In fact, plenty do. But for now, let's go with the obvious and say it is Katzev and the rest of the syndicate. They're hell-bent on revenge because you killed Laurent. You're hell-bent on revenge because they killed Alex and almost got you. How can I help?"

"I need to know where Katzev lives."

"I have no idea."

"Best guess?"

"Probably Manhattan. Maybe Milan. Could be Paris. Hell, it could be Russia, since he obviously loves the motherland enough to associate himself with it. Or Scotland, since he is, after all, Scottish. What I'm saying is that he could be anywhere.

Whenever I've dealt with him, it's been through a secure line. I was offered the job, we negotiated the price, I received half the money the next day, and the rest of money was wired to me when the job was done. I assume it's been the same for you."

"It has. But you have connections, Vincent. Everywhere. You must know someone who knows where he lives."

"I know a few people who might know, but I can't give you their names, Carmen. That's not how I work. You know that."

"Then leave it up to them," she said. "Would you call them and give them my number? If they choose to help me, that's their decision. This way, you haven't compromised anyone. It'll be on them to call and decide if they wish to get involved. You know I won't say anything if they agree to help me. That's not how *I* work."

"I know it isn't."

"Will you make the calls?"

"I'll make the calls."

"I appreciate it, Vincent."

"It might not be Katzev or the syndicate, Carmen. You need to consider every job you've ever done. I know that's a daunting task, but you need to do it and you need to think who else might be targeting you. You have to figure out how someone suddenly found you in Bora Bora, of all places, when you've had a place there for years. After all this time, how did they find you now? This stinks of something recent. Have you looked into Alex's life? Did he slip up and talk to someone? If he did, who did he talk to? And who did that person talk to?"

She felt a chill and looked down the long corridor that led to the bar, where Jake was waiting for her. He mentioned that he spoke to Alex before they left for the island. Who did he speak to after that?

"I have to go," she said. "I'll take everything into consideration. You'll make the calls?"

"I said I would."

"I appreciate it."

"Watch your back, Carmen. Keep an open mind. And stay in touch. I'll do what I can from afar."

CHAPTER FOUR

She hurried down the corridor, hoping she was wrong but knowing in her gut that she was right. She rounded the corner and looked for him at the bar. He was gone. So were their drinks. The bartender caught her eye and held up a piece of paper for her.

She had no time for this. She had to get out of here now, while she still had a chance, but she needed to know what he wrote to her since it might inform what she did next. She walked over to the bartender, a stocky man somewhere in this thirties whose dark hair was slicked back in such a way that it revealed a handsome face.

"My husband," she said. "How long ago did he leave?"

"Ten minutes? He wanted me to give you this."

She took the note and opened it. Five words inside: "Sorry. I had no choice."

She looked behind her, saw nothing out of the ordinary then turned back to the bartender. "Did you happen to see him use his phone?"

"I did."

So, he called ahead. Or they called him. Either way, he told them she was here. But why? If they wanted her dead, he could have shot her an hour ago.

Because they want to bring you in.

It was possible, but why? She was partly responsible for Laurent's death. Did they want to have their way with her before they killed her? Katzev might want to do the job himself. She could see that happening. Or they might think she has information she shouldn't have access to, though she didn't know what that could be.

She needed to leave, but she couldn't go out the front entrance. Not even the side. Soon, this place would be surrounded by them, if it wasn't already.

"Your husband said you had fifteen minutes," the bartender said. "I'm not sure what he meant by that, but it might mean something to you."

"It does." Why was he tipping her off? Was he forced into this? Or was it to make her feel a false sense of security? With five minutes on her side, she might think she could get out now and escape them, when in reality, they'd be right outside waiting for her. This could be a trap. "I didn't see him leave. Which way did he go?"

"He asked if he could use the service exit. Sounds strange, but I've had stranger requests. We accommodated him."

Trap. "I see."

He paused. She could feel him studying her. "Are you in some sort of trouble, Miss?"

Use him.

"I am."

"What kind of trouble?"

"I told my husband I was leaving him tonight. He told me I wasn't and that he'd make sure of it. You know what that means. He's abusive. He's had me dealt with before and he's going to do it again."

"Is there anything I can do?"

"Can you get me into a room?"

"You'd need to check in—"

"You asked if you could help. I need to get into a room right now. He's called people to come here and reason with me, if you get my drift."

"Miss—"

"It's important."

"I don't have that authority."

"Then do you have some place I could hide? A storage area? A conference room I can step into?"

"For how long?"

"An hour? Men are going to come here. They're going to ask if you've seen me. I need you to tell them that I left the moment you gave me the note. If they harass you, tell them you'll call the police. They'll leave if you say that. They won't want any trouble."

"Why don't we just call the police now?"

"Because they won't get here in time. My husband left quickly for a reason. He used the service exit for a reason. This note is a threat."

He looked at the note in her hand, then down the length of the bar, where another bartender was restocking glasses while glancing in their direction. "Phil, give me a minute, OK?"

The man looked at Carmen, then back at the bartender. "We're closing in forty-five, Jon."

"I said a minute. I'll be back."

* * *

He led her to an area behind the bar. They started walking down a short hallway that led to a set of swinging doors.

"Just go with this," he said. "Act natural."

They entered the kitchen, which was large and shiny due to the bright lights glinting off the stainless steel tables, racks, and appliances. Carmen glanced around for cameras in the ceiling, but it was so vast and Jon was moving so quickly, she didn't notice any. She counted six people in the kitchen. They turned a corner and she counted a seventh, all of whom were either cleaning up for the night or doing prep for the following morning's breakfast service. Another sweep of the room. It unnerved her that she saw no cameras because she knew better.

"Everybody," he said. "This is my girlfriend, Lisa. She just got some bad news and needs a space where she can be alone. My shift is up in forty-five.

Does anyone mind if she hangs out in the stairwell until I'm finished?"

"I thought you were gay."

"Funny, Mac. Are we good, everyone?"

Shrugs all around.

"Thanks."

He took her by the hand, they cut left and pushed through another set of doors. Below her was a staircase. Is this where he brought Jake? She turned to him and asked.

"It is, but don't worry about it. The door below is bolted shut. No one can get in here and they won't think you're back here. So, stay here. I'll work on getting you a room."

"Threaten them with the police when they come. Get them out."

"I'll do my best."

"Thank you," she said.

"You'll be fine. If they're coming, they're going to want to see me behind the bar. I'll be back."

He turned to leave.

Each door had a small square window that looked into the kitchen. As she watched him go, every set of eyes in that kitchen turned to her.

Carmen stepped away from the windows, incredulous that she was in this position.

A simple walk in Manhattan to clear her head had turned into this? She was thinking how unreal the past two hours had been when her cell phone rang. She reached into her coat pocket and pulled it out. A number she didn't recognize. Private caller.

She hesitated before she answered it. "Hello?"

A man's voice. Soft, almost fragile. "Carmen Gragera?"

She didn't respond.

"It's all right, Carmen. I'm a friend of Vincent's. He called a moment ago and told me you are in something of a bind."

She closed her eyes in relief.

"Would you like some help?" he asked.

"I would."

"Are you able to come to me now?"

"I'm in the middle of a situation."

"I see. Is there anything I can do?"

"I can handle this. Would you be able to meet tomorrow?"

"Tomorrow's fine."

"I appreciate it."

"It's my pleasure. I'm old, Carmen. You probably can hear it in my voice. I don't leave the house much anymore, but don't let that worry you. I live for my calls from Vincent. He keeps me alive with them. Reminds me why I once was on top and still matter now. Name your time."

"Morning?"

"Ten?"

"Perfect."

He gave her his address.

"What's your name?" she asked.

The line went dead.

* * *

When his shift was over and the bar was closed, the bartender, Jon, returned. He looked tense and on edge, but also in control. His eyes reminded her of her Alex's—big and blue. Intelligent and intense.

"Did they come?" she asked.

"They came."

"How many?"

"Four."

"What happened?"

"They asked for you. I told them that you left. They said that was impossible. I told them you returned five minutes after your husband left and that you probably went to find him."

"Did they buy it?"

"I don't know. But they left. And I have this for you." He held out a card for her. It was a key to a room. "Follow me."

* * *

"We'll use the service elevators," he said as they pushed through the swinging doors. They went to the rear of the kitchen, crossed through another set of doors, and came upon a bank of elevators. "These are used for room service. We can access any room from here."

"I can't tell you how much I appreciate this."

He pressed a button. "My mother went through the same sort of shit with my father. I was too young to do anything about it. I'm glad to help."

"How much do I owe you?"

"Nothing."

The doors slid open and they stepped inside. He pressed the button marked *29*, the doors whisked shut, and the elevator started its ascent.

"The room wasn't free," she said. "I plan to pay for it."

"Actually, it is free. I had it comped for you. I told them that I spilled a drink on you and that you asked for a room so you could clean up. We're not full. It's not a big deal. They'll treat this like any check-in. You'll need to be out by noon tomorrow."

"I'll be long gone by then," Carmen said.

The elevator slowed. The doors slid open and they stepped into a small waiting area before they turned into a warmly lit hallway.

Her room was at the far end of the hall. When they reached it, he slid the key into the slot, unlocked the door, and they stepped inside. Carmen was expecting something nice—it was the Waldorf, after all—but she wasn't expecting a corner suite with two stunning views of the city.

She went over to the windows and looked down at Park, where traffic was light. At some point, it had started to rain. The streets were shiny and bright. Jake's face flashed before her eyes.

Where are you? she wondered.

"The bathroom is through there," Jon said. "You'll find a robe and toiletries. Extra pillows are in this closet. I also comped you on room service, so if you're hungry in the morning, indulge yourself. Get the blinis with caviar. You won't regret it."

"You're very kind," she said.

"It was my pleasure, Carmen."

"Would you like a drink? I'm sure there's something in the fridge." She went to the small refrigerator that was tucked beneath the work desk and opened it. "And there is. They have everything. Would you care to join me? Vodka?"

He walked over to the door and put his hand on the doorknob. "I should be leaving."

"I'm sorry," she said. "You've probably been on your feet for hours."

She smiled as she crossed the distance between them. She looked into his blue eyes and was about to shake his hand when she reached up, grabbed each side of his head, and jerked it so sharply his neck broke.

There was no struggle. Just surprise in his eyes before they became dilated with death. He slumped forward and fell hard at her feet. His legs quivered for a moment, a rush of air escaped his lungs, and then he went still.

She looked down at him. "I never told you my name, Jon, so they must have told you. And that means they also know where I am." She shook her head at him. "What a waste. Are they waiting for you downstairs? Of course, they are. I bet they're waiting for you to return so you can bring them up here. Then you'd be expecting the rest of the money they promised you. That's where you weren't thinking. You've seen their faces. Already, you know too much. They would have killed you even if I hadn't. Then they'd leave here with me."

She put her hand in her coat pocket, felt the Glock, and edged open the door. No one in the hallway. The service elevators were straight ahead of her, but they were at the opposite end of the hall.

She didn't know how she'd do it, but she needed to leave before they came on their own. She pulled Jon's keys out of his pants pocket, left the room, and started moving quickly toward the elevators, listening for any sign of someone coming her way. On one level, she wished that was the case. That way, she could take the stairs, bypass them, and grab another elevator on another floor.

But they were waiting for him. They needed him—at least for now. How long would they wait before they decided something was wrong? Ten minutes? Fifteen? If she were them, that's how long she'd wait. Then she'd worry. Then she'd act.

At the service elevator they'd been in earlier, she tried three keys from his keychain before she found the correct one, turned it in the lock, and was able to press the down button. The doors slid open, suggesting that no one had used the elevator since they left it. She stepped inside and pressed *K* for kitchen. The elevator plunged.

She tried to still her nerves, but it was difficult. How would she get out of here? Some of them would be waiting in the bar area, while others would be guarding the building's exits. She looked up at the dial and her mind raced while the floors sped by. Soon, she'd be next to a room filled with kitchen staff. If they saw her, they wouldn't just question why she was there again. They'd also want to know why she wasn't with Jon. What would she say if someone asked? Worse, because Jon had escorted her so quickly through the kitchen, her scan of the place was too brief to see if there were any cameras tucked in the corners. She didn't know if she was about to be on surveillance or not, but if there were cameras in the kitchen and depending on where they were located, she could be.

The elevator slowed. The doors slid open to the sounds of talking, laughter, the clatter of trays, and the clinking of glassware and silverware. With the bar and restaurant closed, the atmosphere was more relaxed than it had been before. The evening was winding down.

Just outside the elevator, she looked up at the ceiling for a camera, but there was none. At least not there. The kitchen was something altogether different. She knew there were cameras in there somewhere. There had to be. The moment she entered that kitchen to escape, she would be recorded as she tried to leave unnoticed. Not that it mattered much. She had walked through the kitchen earlier. They already had her on tape.

She held the elevator doors open and looked left, saw her first obstacle, and also noted how fleeting her anonymity would be.

The doors to the service elevators were now open. The interior room was no longer private.

A man standing at a stainless steel table with a butcher knife in his hand looked up at her. Medium height. Blondish hair. Maybe forty. On the muscular side.

In spite of the kitchen noise, he must have heard the elevator doors slide open. He was wearing a white uniform spattered with blood. The ends of the sleeves were wet with it. On his head was a tall chef's hat. It was pristine in ways that the rest of him wasn't.

On the table were several long tubes of whole filets encased in plastic wrap. To his left were stacks of freshly cut steaks, unwrapped. Earlier, when Jon led her through the kitchen, she hadn't noticed him, so it was unlikely that he had any context of who she was or that Jon had called out to the group that she was his girlfriend and that he was helping her.

Their eyes met. There was a moment when it appeared that he was going to put the knife down on the table. But he didn't. This was Manhattan, after all. To him, she was an intruder, someone who had no business being here. So, why was she here? And how did she get inside that elevator without the required key?

He came around the table with the knife at his side and a questioning look on his face.

She stepped out of the elevator and moved into the interior room.

"Can I help you?" he asked.

She put a finger to her lips, removed the Glock from her coat pocket and pointed it at him. "Maybe," she said. "Let's find out."

CHAPTER FIVE

She motioned for him to come inside the room. For a moment, he didn't move. Then he took a long look at that gun and decided that he better.

Carmen stepped back to minimize the chance of being seen by others. "Back here," she said. "With me."

He moved closer.

"If you cooperate, I won't kill you. If you do something stupid, I'll take everyone out." She nodded at the butcher knife. "Put it down."

He hesitated, but then did as he was told. He put it down on one of the empty carts next to him.

She looked beyond him into the kitchen. It was only a matter of time before someone walked over and spotted them.

Move.

"I need a jacket like yours," she said. "Not clean. Filthy. And I'll need a hat. Can you find something that will fit me?"

"No."

"Why?"

"There's a laundry chute in the locker room. At the end of our shifts, we drop our whites into it."

"Then step into the elevator. I'll have to use what you're wearing."

Here, just off the kitchen, a key wasn't necessary to open the elevator doors, so she pressed a button. The doors beside her slid open. She cocked her head toward the empty elevator and he stepped inside. She put her foot in front of the right door to block them from closing while keeping her gun trained on him.

He took off his chef's hat, then started to unbutton his jacket, which went just above his knees. "It's too large for you," he said.

"I'm not going for couture."

That stopped him and he looked at her with new eyes. For him, humor was unexpected in a situation such as this, but then he didn't know Carmen or how she viewed the world.

She started to twist her hair into a chignon, which was difficult considering she was holding a loaded gun. Still, she'd done it before and she did it now. It wasn't exactly as neat as her mother taught her when Carmen was a teen in Spain, but in this situation, it would do.

He handed her the jacket, which had the coppery scent of blood on it. "I assume you want the hat?" he asked.

"I do."

He gave it to her.

"Step back," she said.

He did and she slipped into the jacket. It was huge on her, but she didn't plan on being seen in it for long. With the gun in her hand, she struggled with the buttons while also keeping an eye on him.

"Why are you doing this?" he asked.

"Don't talk."

"It's a simple question."

If she told him, it might keep him quiet for another minute, which is all she needed. "There are people here who want to kill me. I need a disguise that will get me out of here. This is as good as it gets."

"Who wants to kill you?"

"Does it matter?"

She put the hat on top of her head, but it was too big. The bonus? It was made of paper. She took it off, folded a section in the back, and ran her bloody sleeve inside the crease. She pressed down and held it for a minute to make sure it would stick. It did, but for how long? Blood was like glue, especially when it started to congeal. She felt it might work, but who knew? There was no certainty in situations such as this. Gently, she put the hat back on her head and this time, it fit.

"I might be able to help you," he said.

"I had a similar offer tonight. Didn't work out."

"Look, if someone here is trying to kill you—"

She stepped forward and swung her gun at him in an arc that was so swift, it connected the butt of her gun against the side of his temple before he knew what hit him.

She could have killed him, but she didn't want to. Unlike Jon, he'd done nothing to betray her. He'd be able to identify her, but so would the hotel's security cameras, which were worse because of the hard evidence they offered. She hadn't seen any cameras, but that meant nothing. She knew that somewhere during her time here, she'd been captured by them.

She reached out and caught him as he fell. She hit him just hard enough to knock him unconscious. She leaned him against the corner of the elevator.

"You'll be all right," she said. "Take a Tylenol when you wake up. Maybe three. And thanks for not making a scene. Most would have."

She turned to the panel behind her and pressed the button that would take him to the forty-seventh floor. She stepped out as the doors slid shut, she heard the elevator lift, and then she turned her attention to the kitchen.

* * *

There was only one way out and it was through the service entrance. Would they be waiting for her there? Absolutely. But they didn't know when she'd come through the door, which gave her the edge.

So did the bloody chef's jacket and hat she was wearing. They wouldn't be expecting her in either of them. The disguise might buy her time, but it wouldn't buy her much. It would take a moment for it to register, but soon enough, they'd recognize her face. And when they did, they'd act. She didn't know what their orders were. Shoot her right there? Bring her in? She had a feeling it was the latter. Katzev would want his say for her part in killing Laurent—if that even was what this was about.

She needed something more. Something that would shake them and distract them.

What she considered was risky, but it might work. She pulled out her cell, which was no ordinary cell. It was a satellite phone, which looked like a cell, only with a thick antenna on top of it. With it, nobody could trace her. She dialed 911 knowing that.

The line rang once. When the dispatcher came on the line, Carmen saw another opportunity. She entered the kitchen with the phone concealing the left side of her face and walked straight across to the double set of doors that led to the stairwell and ultimately to the service entrance. People along the periphery. Her step was relaxed, not rushed. Nobody stopped her. Nobody said anything.

But the dispatcher was talking.

"What's your emergency?" the woman repeated.

Carmen waited for the doors to swing shut behind her before she descended the stairs and told her about the tragedy she'd just come upon.

* * *

At the base of the stairs was the door Jon told her about earlier. It was bolted shut, but she had his keys. After several tries, she found the right one and then waited for the sound of sirens to arrive outside.

It took five minutes and when they came, they arrived in force, as she knew they would. She did, after all, call in a triple homicide.

She told the dispatcher that there were multiple stabbings on the sidewalk between St. Bartholomew's Church on Park and Fiftieth Street. "You'll find them on Fiftieth," she said breathlessly to the dispatcher. "Right across the street from the Waldorf. Three people on the sidewalk. I think they were robbed. One might still be alive. Please, hurry!"

She waited until she was sure the police were there and then she unlocked the door and stepped out.

It was still raining.

The night sky was alive with the sound of sirens and the rapid movement of flashing lights. People were gathering. Some—the cops—were shouting.

Ahead of her, on the sidewalk, were two hulking men. Both in black. She looked left and right. Saw cops checking the street. Saw bellhops and valet drivers watching the action. Saw one of the two brutes turn to look at her. Dismiss her. Then turn to look at her again. She saw him nudge his partner's arm as she walked to the street, which now was clogged with traffic. A cop was preventing any movement from going forward. This was a potential crime scene. Another cop was on Park, where the traffic was moving.

She started to walk toward him.

The two men watched her. Her hand was on her Glock. Her heart hammered in her chest, not so much out of fear but because of the thrill of knowing that she had outwitted them.

As she walked near them, she looked at each of them. Recognized one of them from a job she did years ago, though she couldn't remember his name. She saw the anger on their faces. The resentment of what she'd created. They knew she set this up. It was as clear as the lights strobing across their pissed-off faces.

"Tell Katzev to fuck off," she said to the one she recognized. "And then tell him to watch his back."

"You're going to die, Carmen."

"You think so?"

"Just a matter of time."

She walked past them. Heard the rain tap against her hat. Wondered if they'd make a move. Wondered if this was it. Without Alex in her life, a part of her didn't care if her time was up. A part of her would be happy to be nailed in the back of the head and go straight into the darkness where Alex would greet her. She missed him that much. More than anything, she wanted to be with him again. But because of what happened to him, a larger part of her wanted very much to stay alive and do what she'd set out to do. She returned to Manhattan for revenge. She planned to make them pay for what they did to him. And to her.

"I guess that's true for each of us," she said over her shoulder. "Katzev is cleaning house. You two might be next. I'd give some thought to that if I were you."

"You won't make it, Carmen."

"Knowing Katzev, you might not either. But look at me. Keep your eyes on my ass, boys. I'm walking away from you right now."

CHAPTER SIX

She awoke the next morning at a Holiday Inn Express on Union Street in Brooklyn. It was a shithole, but it was next to the subway and it was out of Manhattan, which was good enough for her.

When she checked in late the night before, the woman at the reception desk said in a drowsy, monotone voice that they were happy she chose the Holiday Inn Express and how wonderful it was to have her there. The rest was just as canned, which Carmen sometimes liked to toy with, especially when she was as stressed as she was then. Verbally boxing with someone relaxed her.

She appraised the woman behind the counter. Dry blonde hair ruined from a kitchen-sink dye job. Heavy red lipstick that drew attention to a chipped front tooth turned yellow from smoking. Heavy makeup that was darker than her natural skin color and that stopped at her jawline. She hadn't blended it down toward her neck. She looked ridiculous. Carmen watched her go through the motions of customer service as if connecting with a customer was the last thing she wanted to do.

Let's see what she's got.

"How was your day?" the woman asked.

"Murderous," Carmen said.

"Sorry to hear that."

"No. Literally, it was murderous."

The woman lifted her eyes to her.

"I can't believe I got through it. It almost killed me."

The woman swiped a card through a machine, tucked it in a small, used envelope that read *Holiday Inn Express*, and went back to the script she'd memorized from years of repeating the same rhetoric.

"We at the Holiday Inn Express want you to know that we have complimentary coffee, juices, and breakfast items in the morning. Our complimentary breakfasts, which are free to our valuable customers, are available from 6 a.m. until 10 a.m. We are known for our cinnamon rolls. You will love them."

"I usually sleep until eleven."

"Then you will miss breakfast."

"You won't hold it for me?"

"We can't do that, ma'am."

"Why?"

"Policy."

"More likely, the proliferation of bacteria."

The woman blinked.

"About the rolls," Carmen said. "I'm allergic to cinnamon. Anything you can do about that?"

"There's fruit."

"No cinnamon-free rolls?"

"Fruit."

"Oranges?"

"I have no idea."

"Grapefruit?"

"I know there's a carousel of cereal."

"A carousel?"

"Four different kinds. You like fruit? We've got Fruit Loops."

"How's the coffee?"

"Hot."

"Does 'hot' mean 'burned'?"

"We don't burn our coffee."

"Can you guarantee that?"

"No."

"Do you have an egg selection?"

"All that's hot is the coffee. And the toast."

"That sounds limited."

"It's complimentary."

"At these prices, it isn't."

"The Holiday Inn Express offers reasonable rates that help you stretch your dollar. Will this be on your credit card?"

"Cash." Carmen gave her the money, took the change, and pocketed the card the woman swiped earlier.

"That's the key to your room."

"I gathered that."

"Fourth floor. Take a right at the elevator. Have a lovely stay."

"Will I see you at breakfast?"

"Excuse me?"

"It's on me. I'd love to sit and talk."

"Have a lovely stay, ma'am."

"I can't imagine I won't."

She didn't, not that that surprised her. If she thought last night that a walk in the city would help to clear her head because she couldn't sleep, then what took place because of that walk made sleep impossible.

Since at least the bath towels smelled of bleach, she covered the top of the bed with them before lying on top it. Spocatti encouraged her to think beyond Katzev and the syndicate. He wanted her to consider all her hits before assuming it was them. She trusted him, so she thought it through.

When she told the men last night to tell Katzev to fuck off, neither looked bewildered at the use of his name. They just fired back at her, which told her two things, neither of which provided a concrete answer. If they were well trained, they wouldn't have reacted at the mention of his name. Let her believe what she wanted to believe, especially if Katzev wasn't involved. On the other hand, if Katzev was behind this, the same was true. Show no knowledge of his name, which they didn't. Doing so would only tip her off.

Is it Katzev?

She didn't know. Before she and Alex left for Bora Bora, they warned the syndicate that if they came after them for killing Laurent, they would send everything they knew about them to the press.

Admittedly, that wasn't much of a threat because the syndicate worked behind a cloak of privacy that was fairly airtight. Katzev and the syndicate knew that. Still, as with any threat—and if they were indeed behind this—they took it seriously, tracked them down, killed Alex and nearly her.

With the syndicate, everything was handled over secure lines. E-mail addresses were constantly changed and associated with accounts in third-world countries. Whenever they paid her for a job, it was from a numbered Swiss bank account with no name attached to it.

In the seven years she'd done jobs for them, she only saw Laurent twice. First, when he courted her to work for them, and then at the end, when she helped to kill him. She'd never seen Katzev or any other members of the syndicate. With the exception of Katzev's fake Russian accent on the other end of a phone, everyone associated with the syndicate was foreign to her.

As much as she respected Spocatti, she knew in her gut that it was Katzev and the rest of the syndicate who were behind this. They had a direct reason to come after both her and Alex. They wanted their revenge for the loss of Laurent and they got it. At least partly.

But how did they learn they were there? If Jake was legit and he was friends with Alex, it was possible that Alex told him where they were going and that Jake sold the information to the syndicate. It also would explain why he sold her out last night.

Start at the beginning.

Before they killed Laurent, why would the syndicate want her and Alex dead? Alex worked with them more often than she did. Did he stumble upon something he shouldn't have? Something that incriminated the syndicate? Did they think he shared the information with her? It was possible, but how did they find out? She knew Alex kept an apartment in the city, but the syndicate also knew that and at this point, she knew they already had gone through it and taken any incriminating evidence. If there was any.

She checked the time. In an hour, she'd meet with Spocatti's elderly, nameless contact. She needed to shower. She'd have to wear the same clothes, but so be it. Until this was resolved, going back to her apartment was out of the question. She needed to set up shop somewhere else, so it might as well be there.

CHAPTER SEVEN

The address he gave her was 118 East Sixty-First Street, which turned out to be a brick-and-limestone townhouse protected by a black iron gate connected to four limestone columns, on top of which were two original iron lamps.

There was a large maple tree in front, which was a few leaves shy of being fully exposed to the waning days of fall, and a doorbell on one of the posts, which she pressed.

She watched the first- and second-story windows for movement, but saw none. After a moment, there was an audible buzzing sound, she opened the gate and stepped down the stairs to the black front door, which opened as she approached it.

Behind it was a middle-aged man with a patch over his eye. But not just any patch. Sewn into the front of it was a working watch, sapphire in color, with a ticking second hand, which caused her to pause before she could collect herself from the surprise of it. He had short graying hair and appeared as tall and as broad as the doorway itself. Clean shaven. Face devoid of emotion. She knew an ex-Marine when she saw one, and she was looking at one now.

"Carmen Gragera?"

She focused on his other eye, which was as blue as the watch's sapphire background. "That's me."

He moved to his right. "Step inside, please."

She did, and then he closed the door and she held out her arms for him in the sunlit entryway. "It's in my jacket pocket," she said as he patted her down. "After last night, I couldn't be on the streets without it. I hope you understand."

"I don't understand anything about what you do. But it isn't my job to judge."

I think you just did.

He took the Glock and continued his search. Even if Spocatti did send her here with his blessing, she felt nervous and naked without her gun. When he was satisfied she carried nothing else on her, he asked if he could take her coat.

She slipped it off and handed it to him. When he took it from her, she noted that his hands were triple the size of hers. Alex was six-foot-two, but this man was much taller. Six-foot-eight? She looked around the wide, aged oak foyer and saw all the delicate antiques on the side tables and walls. On this level, the ceilings were high. Probably twelve feet.

She bet he was happy for the extra space.

"This way," he said, motioning in front of him. "Mr. Gelling is waiting for you in the library."

Gelling? The name meant nothing to her.

"And your name?" she asked.

"Mr. Gelling will decide if you need access to that information. Follow me, please."

Jesus.

She followed him down a long hallway and past a beautifully designed living room that had the sort of furnishings that suggested either Gelling came from money or he knew exactly what to do with it when he earned it himself.

On a round mahogany table in the center of the room was a Lalique Bacchantes vase. Just from the depth of its opalescence alone, Carmen knew it was an original made by Rene Lalique himself.

The current revivals the company made were beautiful, but inferior. Some thought they looked like frosted glass. But this was the real thing from the late twenties, something she'd only ever seen in a museum. With its graceful series of nudes surrounding the vase, it was the epitome of the Art Nouveau movement she loved so much. She was a long way from her days as an art history major in Spain, but the bug hadn't left her. A part of her wanted to go over and admire the vase. She wanted to touch it.

But Big Ben was having none of that. There was no slowing him down. Soon, they were in the library and she faced Gelling, an ancient-looking man with a full head of white hair neatly combed back and an inquisitive face that brightened when he saw her. In his plush, battery-powered wheelchair, he buzzed quickly toward her.

"Carmen Gragera," he said in a voice that wasn't as frail as it was when she spoke to him last night on the phone. "I'm so glad you came."

"Thank you for seeing me."

He stopped just short of her and looked up at her with clouded green eyes that reminded her of the sea. He reached out his hand and she shook it. Here is where she felt his frailty. His skin was soft and papery. His fingers, twisted from arthritis, were so slender, she knew she could snap them with a brisk shake. On the back of his hands were brown spots and purple bruises. It reminded her of her grandfather's hands not long before he died.

"My name is Gelling," he said. "James Gelling. It's a pleasure to meet you. I've heard about you, you know?"

"I didn't know."

"Vincent thinks a lot of you."

"I'm glad to hear that. It's mutual. I've learned a lot from him."

"Take it all in, my dear. Take it all in. He's the best. You've worked with him only once, correct? That Wall Street job?"

"That's right."

"Didn't go as planned, I hear."

"Sometimes, it doesn't."

He waved his crippled hand in the air. "So many things don't. Look at me, for instance. Pretzels for fingers. Trapped in this wheelchair. A slave to its batteries, not to mention to my own body, which has betrayed me worse than my own children did." He cocked his head at her. "All of them are dead, you know? I outlived them all. Every last one. Isn't that unusual? And wonderful, given how they treated me. How old do you think I am?"

She knew better than to stretch the truth with this man. She studied his face and gave it her best shot. "In your nineties?"

"High or low end?"

"Depends on how young you were when you had your children."

"I'm not saying."

"Then I'm thinking somewhere in the middle."

"So, I've done well," he said. "The lotions worked. And you've fed my vanity, which doesn't happen often enough. I'm one hundred and three years old, Carmen. I could be gone during this very meeting, so you should prepare yourself for that. I could just slump over in my chair, shit my pants, and that's it. Lights out. That's what it's like at my age. You never know when death will hit. Being this old is the most surreal experience. I go to sleep at night and think, 'Well, that's it. Surely, I've snuffed the final candle by now.' Then I wake the next morning stunned to realize I have another shot to make a difference."

"How do you make a difference?" she asked.

"In all sorts of ways. I believe one of them is the reason you're here. Come, come. Over to those sofas behind me. Have a seat in one of them. If I'm going to help you, I want to get to know you better. I want to know about you."

She felt her guard go up. Carmen rarely spoke about her personal life. Since her early twenties, the only person she fully let in was Alex.

He whizzed over in his chair, which whirred past her as if a gigantic bee had been let loose in the room. She sensed he enjoyed the speed. Got a little thrill from it. "Would you like something to drink? Iced tea? Coffee?"

"I'd love an iced tea."

"Lemon? No lemon?"

"Lemon."

"Sweetened? Unsweetened."

"Unsweetened."

"I figured as much. You're trim." He looked up at her friend, Big Ben with the watch eye patch, who was standing beside the sofa in which she sat, his massive forearms folded across the broad expanse of his equally massive chest. "An unsweetened ice tea with lemon for Carmen and the same for me, please. Don't forget my straw. And stop looking so tense, Frank. Carmen is a friend of Vincent's and thus she's a friend of ours. We're just going to chat for a bit before we get down to it." He lowered his voice and spoke to Frank as if she wasn't there. "I'm curious to know how she became an assassin."

When Frank left, Gelling looked at Carmen and said, "Did the watch render you useless for a moment?"

"I'm not sure about useless. But I've never seen anything like it."

"Frank's an eccentric."

"I'd finger him as a former Marine."

"And you'd be correct. But the watch," he whispered. "I think it gives him an edge. It catches people off guard. You wouldn't believe the situations it's helped him out of. He's a beast of a man, of course, but when he appears, what people see first is the watch. They can't help but stare at it. It's actually very shrewd of him. It allows him that additional moment to act. You should try it?"

"I prefer my Glock to a clock."

"Clever. So? Back to you. How did you fall into that line of work? You don't look the type."

You haven't seen me cut a man's throat.

"Mr. Gelling..." she said.

"I understand. You're uncomfortable talking about how your past led to your present. Many of you are. But to help you, I need to know you. Not everything. But as a former psychiatrist, I'm naturally curious. How does one choose a career of delivering death? What happened in their lives to make such a decision—and then to master the craft? You don't need to give me every gory detail, Carmen, but if you want me to help you find Katzev, which I can, I do expect you to play nice and tell me how you got to where you are now."

At first, she didn't speak. It was unnatural for her to share such intimate information with a stranger. Even Vincent didn't know anything about her personal life—he never asked, likely because she'd turn the tables and ask him how he got involved in the business. But looking at Gelling and his growing impatience, she knew she had no choice if he was going to help her. "My father was an assassin," she said. "I learned from him."

"What a curious inheritance. When was this?"

"When I graduated college."

"What did you study?"

"Art history."

"Well, there's a stretch. From Matisse to murder. That would be fun to read on a resume. Did you always know about your father's line of work?"

"I didn't."

"What did you think he did for work?"

"I was told that he worked as a corporate consultant. Turns out that was true, only when I found out what he was consulting them on, it wasn't exactly as innocent as it sounded at the time."

"How did you find out?"

"I was abducted."

She watched Gelling's face light up again. He was enjoying the story. It didn't matter to him that reliving that time in her life was painful for her. If Spocatti hadn't sent her here, she'd leave.

"By whom?" he asked.

"Men my father was hired to kill. They caught wind of it—don't ask me how, because I don't know—and they came after me. I was working at the Met at the time. I used to walk part of the way home, especially in the fall, because for me, this is the best time of year to be in Manhattan. I was on Fifth. They pulled alongside me in a limousine, held a gun on me, told me to get inside, and took me hostage. They warned my father that if he didn't allow them to leave the States and go back to their country, where they stupidly thought they'd be safe, they would kill me. My father agreed. I was released. They got on a plane and went home. My father waited two months, hopped on a plane, and killed them in Stockholm."

"It's always Stockholm," he said. "Or Berlin or Beirut. Or Moscow or Madrid, but never Brisbane. Never Canada. Never Maine. How those areas must feel slighted by assassins."

She just stared at him.

"How did you feel when you knew who your father was?"

"Betrayed." She paused and thought back to that time. Now, Carmen was thirty-eight. She was twenty-three when she was abducted. Had it really been fifteen years since she first learned the truth about her father? She was surprised by how quickly the time had passed, and also by how much she had changed during that time. "But also relieved. He saved my life."

"But only after he put it in jeopardy."

"Indirectly, but you're right."

Gelling was about to speak when Frank entered the room with the iced teas. The room's bright sunlight reflected off the watch, making it appear like a sphere. Carmen wondered if it glowed in the dark.

Frank stopped beside them. Gelling's tea had a straw in it with an extendable tip. When the drinks were delivered, he shooed the man away.

"During those two months, you and your father must have talked."

"We did. And I'm not going to lie to you. There's no question I felt betrayed, but I also became intrigued by his life. I always considered my father a gentleman. He wasn't violent. He was nondescript, just an average-looking man who happened to have superior skills in areas that were foreign to me. I was a young woman when I first learned about his other life. My father and I were never very close. After the abduction, I knew why. We began to talk. He told me stories and let me in. Because I didn't judge him, I think part of him wanted to share his life with someone, because he'd never had the opportunity to do so with anyone else."

"He didn't share it with your mother?"

"We never discussed my mother. She left us when I was four."

"Why did she leave?"

"You'd need to ask her."

"Do you keep in touch?"

"Mr. Gelling, I don't even know if she's alive."

"Where is your father now?"

"In a Madrid cemetery."

"See?" he said. "Madrid. It always comes back to one of the big foreign cities. Everything happens there." He leaned toward his glass of iced tea and puckered his lips around the straw. He sipped it while he studied her. "Did he die of natural causes?"

"He was gunned down in the streets of Mexico City."

"Mexico City," he said, as if he was underscoring his former point, which she found pointless. "Awful, but not a surprise. When was this?"

"Fourteen years ago. I was twenty-four."

"And you sought revenge?"

"He was my father. I loved him. Someone had to pay."

"Did you find whoever killed him?"

"I did. I also found the others who targeted him. I killed them all."

"That was a brave undertaking."

"I was twenty-four. I didn't know any better."

"Youth can be so liberating and dangerous. For you, I'm assuming it was both. Why did they want your father dead?"

"He was hired to take out the leader of a drug cartel. The cartel wasn't happy about that. They came after him. The end."

"And then you went into the family business?"

"You could say that. Everything changed for me after my father's death. I saw a different world. I discovered I was a crack shot. The people who used to hire my father contacted me. They offered me a job for an obscene amount of money. The person I was asked to kill was about as close to evil as you could imagine. He hurt people. I suppose that's why I took it. Maybe I thought by getting rid of him, I was doing some good in the world. Maybe that was my justification. But you're right—that's youth for you. Liberating and dangerous. Now I work for hire. My only exception is that I refuse to kill children. I haven't looked back since."

"Not until Alex…"

Just hearing his name stung. The image of his face flashed before her eyes. The ache of his loss was like a tide closing in, suffocating her. She remembered the first time he told her he loved her but then forced the memory away. *Focus.* "Actually, Alex makes me look forward," she said. "They'll pay for what they did to him."

"I don't blame you."

I don't care if you do. "I need your help. I need to know how to get to Katzev."

"Your story is fascinating, Carmen."

"I don't see it that way."

"I do. And I want to thank you for sharing it with me."

You gave me no choice.

"I have one question?"

"What's that?"

"Why won't you kill children? A life is a life. Who cares if it belongs to a child?"

"A conscience needs to begin somewhere, Mr. Gelling."

"That's a smooth answer, Carmen, but I think it goes deeper. Do you have a child?"

She didn't want to go there, but this wasn't about her. It was about Alex. It was about doing anything to avenge his death, so she leveled her eyes with his and told the truth. "I can't have children."

"What a shame. Or not. In my case, I wish I never had children. Rotten little greedy beasts. Still, why can't you have them? Can't conceive?"

"That's right. Years ago, when I was in love with a young man I worked with at the Met, we tried to get pregnant. We were seriously involved for about a year at that point. Neither of us wanted marriage, but children? We both wanted children. Unfortunately, each time we tried, I miscarried. Three times in a row to be exact. I saw my doctor and was told I couldn't carry. Apparently, something's wrong with my tubes. So, life cheated me out of having a child. I have no interest in cheating others out of what I wanted, but couldn't have. Whenever asked, I refuse to do it. There are no exceptions."

"I'm sorry for your losses."

"That was a long time ago."

"But it's still there, isn't it?"

It was with her every day, but she was finished with this line of questioning and sipped her tea, offering no response.

"This Katzev," he said. "Of course, I've heard of him. And also of Jean-Georges Laurent and what you and Alex did to him that night at the Four Seasons."

"Laurent tried to kill us."

"I know he did. And I have to say, what he had in mind was ingenious. Under different circumstances, I think even you would admit to that. But you and Alex were smart to come clean with each other when you did. Love saved you. By telling the truth, you spared each other's lives. It's like a movie."

"How do you know this?"

"It's what I do, Carmen. It's what keeps me going at one hundred and three. People talk to me and tell me things. I'd never tell you who told me anything, of course. That goes back to my days as a psychiatrist. Confidentiality is critical, which is why Vincent trusts me and why you will come to trust me."

He leaned forward in his chair and met her gaze. "Just as you would never kill a child, I would never sell either of you out. We all have our morals and ethics, regardless of how far they're sometimes stretched. I believe that doing the right thing is important. What Laurent and Katzev tried to pull on you and Alex crosses the line. So, here I am. Prepared to help."

She was growing impatient with him. She just bared part of her soul to him. Now, she wanted the address. "Where does Katzev live?"

"I have no idea."

It was like a slap across her face. She was confused. Then angry. She just spilled some of her most personal secrets to this man. "But I thought you knew? Spocatti sent me to you because you knew."

"That isn't true. He sent you here because I know people who might know. In fact, I know people who likely will know because I know everyone. That's what you're really here for, Carmen—my contacts. I'm going to give you a name of a person who I'm fairly certain will know Katzev's address. Or can find it. She's powerful. Travels in all sorts of circles, some of which she'd rather keep quiet, not that I blame her. Odd woman, really, if you know her history, but that's the sort of person you need right now. Someone with her history. And her contacts. And her knowledge of these sorts of things, of which she's intimate. I've already called ahead to tell her about you. She's eager to meet because she thrives on this as much as I do."

"What's her name?"

"Babe McAdoo. She's a socialite from one of the big New York families. Nontraditional. A bit off. As eccentric as, uh, you know who." He glanced quickly at Big Ben. "But in her set, maybe that's just how it is. Who knows with her? There will be times when you'll think she's speaking in tongues, but it's all an act. When you get down to business with her, she's all business. It's like she switches on a light and becomes the person you need. And when she's that person, she's quite good. I actually admire her when she's that person."

"Her name sounds familiar to me."

"McAdoo Seasonings? That's her family."

"I think I've put her on turkey."

"That's a curious way to put it, but in a way, I suppose all of America has. She's been spread from coast-to-coast. And her reach goes beyond the salt-and-pepper set, for which I'm certain she's grateful. Why limit yourself when there are so many other things that can be crushed, blended, and sprinkled?"

"Can I trust her?"

"I wouldn't send you there if you couldn't."

"When should I see her?"

He looked across the room at Frank, who stood in front of a fireplace, above which was a large mirror. "What time is it, Frank?"

"Just after eleven, sir."

"That was quick. Did the mirror help?"

"Yes, sir."

Gelling looked at Carmen. "I adore him. You should see Babe now. She lives on Park. I'll give you her address. And please, after you speak with her, if you could call me? Or even call and stop by afterward? I'd appreciate it. I like to keep up." For an instant, she saw a flash of vulnerability cross his face. A hint of fear. "Knowing how things are proceeding. That's what keeps me going. It's what makes me want to see tomorrow."

CHAPTER EIGHT

Babe McAdoo lived in a townhouse on Seventy-Fourth and Park. Given the long history of her family's seasonings, which Carmen knew were popular in the States, especially around the holidays, when everything is breaded, roasted, dusted, and stuffed, the building was large and stately, one of those rare Manhattan mansions that you stopped to marvel at due to its sheer size and beauty.

Carmen didn't want to be on the street longer than necessary. She walked up a wide set of granite stairs that led to two massive, lacquered mahogany doors, which gleamed in the sun as if they'd just been polished. She rang the doorbell and waited for someone to answer. When the door opened, an older man in a black suit looked out at Carmen with cool dismissal.

She knew it was because of the way she was dressed. And that her hair was a mess because she had no product with her at the Holiday Inn Express. And that she wore no makeup for the same reason. She probably looked a hot wreck. She felt him judge her in that instant and had to stop him when he started to close the door. He thought she was a transient.

"Excuse me," she said. "I'm Carmen Gragera. I have an appointment to see Ms. McAdoo."

His eyes widened. "*You're* Carmen Gragera?"

"I had a rough night."

"Apparently. I apologize for closing the door. Too many people stop by to ask for money. They come in droves. I thought—"…"

That I was a bum. "That's fine," she interrupted. "I know you're probably used to seeing something quite different when someone comes to visit Ms. McAdoo. Women in Chanel. Birkins. Skin lifted so far, it's surprising they don't have beards. That sort of thing."

"I'm afraid, I am." He opened the door for her. "Please come in. And forgive my manners. Ms. McAdoo is expecting you. I assume you're carrying?"

She motioned toward her pocket and he removed her gun.

"It will be kept in a safe spot," he said, putting it in his jacket pocket. "And the rest of you?"

She held out her arms. "There's nothing more, but feel free to search."

He did. Satisfied, he said, "If you'd follow me to the parlor, you can have a seat while I gather her for you."

Gather her for me? Am I dealing with another invalid? "If now isn't a good time—"

"She's just upstairs doing her Turtle Breathing."

"I'm sorry?"

"Her Turtle Breathing."

"I don't understand."

"It's part of her Zen workout. After twenty minutes of Naval Chakra, she always ends with a technique called Turtle Breathing. When she arrives, you'll find her quite relaxed." He paused and reconsidered his statement. "Well, as relaxed as Ms. McAdoo can be. I've never seen a person with such energy. It's...inspiring."

The way he said *inspiring* made it sound exhausting.

They went to the parlor, which seemed as if it was sheathed in gold. Gold-colored wallpaper. Deep gold curtains with massive gold tassels at the five floor-to-ceiling windows facing the street. A sprawling gold Aubusson rug stretched across the parquet floors. Intricately carved gold moldings at the ceilings.

For punches of color, Babe McAdoo placed a black Steinway grand by the front windows; large paintings on the walls circled the room; and four bright red Victorian chairs, upholstered in crushed velvet, were at the room's center, facing each other with a marble-topped coffee table between them. There was more, but as much as she wanted to, she didn't want to take all of it in. She wanted to get to work.

And yet as Carmen sat in one of the uncomfortable chairs, that part of her that admired all that surrounded her couldn't help but look and assess. What she saw was the real deal, much of it seemed untouched. Looking around, she thought a lot of people must have an enthusiastic need for

McAdoo Seasonings, because what she noted—from the painting of water lilies by Monet to the authentic Tiffany lamp on the table beneath it—couldn't have been in their collection otherwise.

There was a disturbance in the air. She heard footsteps coming down the grand set of stairs she saw in the entryway. Then a voice. "Something wet," she heard a woman say. "Something that pops on the tongue. A spritz of fantastic. And maybe crackers. Or something like that. Figure it out. It's what you do best, Max. Five minutes. Is she in there?"

"She is, madam."

"I'm dying to meet her. I *need* this. My body *craves* this. It's been too long. Also get some cheese. She might be hungry. I heard she had a hell of a night last night, poor girl. Sprinkle the cheese with the McAdoo lime chile pepper powder. My blend—not the diluted one we shuck on the shelves. It'll give it a zing. Not too much, though. I don't want to blow her head off."

"Madam..."

"Poor choice of words, I know."

"She's right through there."

"Five minutes, Max. Not a moment longer. You know how I can be after the Turtle Breathing."

"Of course. Five minutes."

"Off you go."

Carmen heard him hurry away. She stood and faced the entrance to the parlor. What came through it was a middle-aged woman, likely near sixty but with some medical assistance, she appeared closer to fifty. Babe McAdoo had dark red hair pulled back into a tight chignon, which revealed a thin, oval face sharpened by years of extreme wealth and all the pressures that came with it. She wore a pale yellow caftan that was so delicate, it made her appear almost ethereal as she moved.

"Hellohoware?" she said, coming across the room with her hand outstretched. "I'm Babe McAdoo. Call me Babe. Everyone does, but only when I invite them to."

"Carmen Gragera," Carmen said. "It's a pleasure."

"Not under these circumstances, I'm afraid. I understand you've been dealt a blow. And that you had a difficult night. And that someone is trying to kill you. And that you need my help. Gelling didn't send you here for just any reason."

"He didn't, though I was under the impression that my conversation with him was private."

"As much as it could be, it was. I don't know any of the particulars, just the generalities. Gelling had to give me something in order for me to agree to see you. I don't see just anyone. He knows that."

Babe McAdoo turned and motioned toward the red chairs. "So, sit," she said. "Right there. That red chair. Let's sit and talk. Let's see what needs to be done and how we can rearrange the chessboard so it's in your favor, not theirs. I *live* for that!"

* * *

After Max returned with the cheese sprinkled with Babe McAdoo's private blend of their lime chile pepper seasoning, the crackers, and two flutes of bubbling champagne, Babe waved him away and lifted her glass to Carmen. "Here's to getting to know one another."

Carmen lifted her glass, touched it against Babe's, and took the smallest of sips. She rarely drank, but she didn't want to offend this woman, who might be able to help her. Still, to get there, they obviously were going to talk, which made her tense.

She already went down memory lane with Gelling. She didn't want to do so again with another stranger.

But she would if that's what it took to get Katzev.

Babe McAdoo surprised her. She leaned back in her red Victorian chair and folded her right leg elegantly over her left. "You're all the same," she said.

"Excuse me?"

"None of you want to talk. That's not a criticism—just an observation. Your privacy means a lot to you. I know it does, for a wealth of reasons, and I get it because my privacy also means a great deal to me because of who I am. I will tell you this, though. I'm no Gelling." She rolled her eyes and took another sip of her champagne. "The psychiatrist in him has a thirst that won't be quenched until his withered heart finally shuts down and his spirit slips through his lips and hopefully through a parted window. Only then, when his energy goes out into the universe and finds more answers to more questions than he ever thought possible, will he truly be happy." She paused. "I think."

She put the glass down on the table between them, put some cheese on a cracker and popped it in her mouth. She closed her eyes and savored it. "When I said that we should get to know each other, I was just being polite. You don't have to share your secrets with me, Carmen. However, I would advise that you tell me those things you think will help us find the person or persons responsible for killing your friend, Alex, and nearly you. Otherwise, what's the point? You'd just be wasting my time, which I can't have. So, yes, you might have to spill a few secrets along the way. You'll feel uncomfortable doing so—I get it—but hopefully it will lead to a successful conclusion. Make sense?"

"I can agree to that."

"Terrific. Have a cracker and some cheese. You look famished. Malnourished. Don't be shy. And if you don't drink, then let's not pretend that you do. What would you like?"

"I'm fine. Really."

"You won't be after my McAdoo lime chile pepper hits your mouth." She called out for Max. "A glass of water, Max. Lemon to freshen it. Make it tall. *Tout suite!*" She returned her attention to Carmen, who was reaching for a cracker and adding a hunk of cheese because, truth be told, she was indeed famished.

"What happened last night?" Babe asked.

Already, Max was coming toward them with a glass of water on a silver tray. A slice of lemon was hooked right on the rim. She took the glass, thanked him for it, ate the cracker and cheese—and immediately went for the water.

"You see," Babe said. "I knew you'd need the water. It's my own blend. We tried to sell it on the shelves, but no one bought it, not that I care. The masses want it bland whereas I like it hot."

Carmen's tongue felt scorched. "Apparently."

"Aren't you Spanish?"

She nodded.

"And that's too spicy for you?"

"It's nuclear."

"It was meant to be. So," she said. "Shall we get down to it? What happened last night?"

Carmen took another drink of water, started at the beginning, and told her in detail.

"So, you killed a man?"

She nodded.

"But you spared another?"

She nodded.

"I have to say, it's ingenious how you threw the other men off. A triple stabbing? Reporting it yourself to the police? Walking away from the men because you knew they couldn't touch you with the police present? This is the stuff for which I live."

"You said that earlier. May I ask why?"

"Because I'm a McAdoo."

"What does that have to do with it?"

Babe sipped her champagne. "I was born into a terminally dull life. When I was young, everything was scripted for me. The family and societal expectations were crushing. My sisters and brothers embraced every bit of it because with it came power and status, which don't interest me. When they were alive, my mother and father reveled in their positions for the same reasons. But not me. I think around the time I was in college, I realized I needed something more, but I didn't know what it was beyond the fact that I needed adventure in my life. Some sort of intrigue that wasn't unlike the mysteries I read. Years later, I found that in a new beau. I learned he was an assassin. Still is, actually. We had a lovely affair. He is far younger than I—I believe he was just starting out at the time—but it didn't matter. As brief as it was, we had a wonderful time together. I was fascinated by what he did for a living. He was fearless and talented. Gifted and bright. We got along famously. Still do. He introduced me to a lot of the people who likely will help us now. Parts of me still live vicariously through him."

Carmen had to ask. "Are you talking about Spocatti?"

"What if I were?" She shrugged dismissively. "Let's get down to it, Carmen. Who do you think is behind all this?"

She told Babe about the syndicate. She told her about what Laurent tried to do to her and Alex, how she and Alex murdered him at the Four Seasons in front of a crowd gathered to celebrate Leana Redman's gift to a suicide prevention organization, and how Alex was murdered at her house in Bora Bora just three weeks later.

"I've never liked those Redmans," Babe said. "Well, at least the majority of them. The way George Redman bulldozed this city to make so much of it his own is disgusting given some of the beautiful old buildings we lost. I do like his daughter, Leana, though. I met her once at a benefit on Anastassios

Fondaras's yacht. She has a spark, that girl. And she's rebellious, which I like. I always thought her father cut her a raw deal, but that's the sort of man he is. He always favored Celina, when I would have taken Leana. You watch. Leana is hungry. She's poised to go places, regardless of who she has to take down to get there."

She saw the patient look on Carmen's face and finished her champagne. "But I digress. This syndicate you talk about—of course, I've heard of it. Over the years, I've met Laurent a few times, though he only warmed to me when he learned I was a McAdoo, which he adored, as so many do for reasons that make my skin crawl. He seemed like a real son of a bitch to me. There was something about him that put me on edge. Then, of course, I found out he was part of this syndicate and my uneasiness about him made sense." She looked at Carmen. "You do know what the syndicate is about, don't you?"

"They've always been secretive with me, but it doesn't take a genius to figure it out. The men and women I was hired to take out were leaders of industry. CEOs. Presidents of corporations. That sort of thing. After a successful hit, I'd wait a few days and then google who replaced the person I killed. Sometimes, I'd learn that the company was put into play because of the sudden lack of leadership. When I learned who benefitted from the hit, I had a better scope of what I was dealing with. The syndicate doesn't comprise only a few people. It comprises many, mostly powerful men and women so ambitious, they'll kill to elevate their positions to the top spot within the company or to take over a company when it's at its most vulnerable."

"Was Laurent the only person you worked with?"

"No. I also worked with a man named Katzev. I believe he's responsible for having Alex and me followed to the island. I don't know that for certain, but I think he wanted to avenge Laurent's death. He got Alex, but not me, which is what last night was all about. Do you know him?"

"I met him years ago."

Carmen couldn't help her surprise. Even *she* hadn't met Katzev. "You did?"

"I did. A long time ago. He's got the accent down, but he's not Russian."

"I hear he's Scottish."

"That's right, but it's difficult to tell, isn't it? In some ways, I think he's worse than Laurent. Nastier, if that's possible."

"How did you know him?"

"Through Laurent. It was only in passing, but I wouldn't want to meet him again. Gave me the creeps. Probably beats women. How certain are you that he's responsible for what happened to Alex?"

"I never could be certain. But my gut says that he is, and my gut has yet to fail me. I rely on it. Beyond that, the facts add up. We killed Laurent. Three weeks later, we were tracked down, Alex was dead, and they almost got me. That can't be a coincidence."

"All of this would seem to point to the syndicate," Babe said. "But what of your other work? You have enemies out there. Have you considered them?"

"Spocatti asked me the same question. I'll be frank with you, Ms. McAdoo—"

"Babe."

"Babe. In any assassin's life, there always will be someone seeking you out. Payback is the nature of the game. Could it be someone else? Sure. But I don't think it is."

Babe leaned forward in her chair. She put the palms of her hands together and pointed her fingers at Carmen. "I don't either," she said. "In fact, I know that Katzev is behind this. Would you like to know how I know?"

Carmen was intrigued by the sudden turn of events. McAdoo knew? "Of course, I would."

"I thought so." Babe turned in her chair. "Max!" she called out. "Bring him in."

CHAPTER NINE

Carmen had been deceived before and wondered if she was being deceived now. Was she calling for Katzev? Did Babe McAdoo join the syndicate so she could have the little side adventures she felt she needed to live a full life? Did she call ahead for him to come, knowing that soon Carmen would be here?

Her mind raced. Spocatti trusted Gelling, which meant he trusted the man's contacts. But at any point, Babe could have deflected, as many did. Had she? She looked at her. The woman was looking over her shoulder, toward the entrance to the room, and seemed at ease. There was a hint of a smile on her lips.

A self-satisfied smile?

Carmen listened to the house and heard footsteps coming from the far end of a hallway she couldn't see. She was seated in the center of the room. The doorway into it was at her far left. Instinctively, she went for her Glock and immediately regretted giving it up when she entered the house.

Babe looked at her. "Don't be frightened," she said. "We're here to help you, Carmen."

"Who is *we*?"

"You'll see."

When she saw, she was speechless. Then instinct took over, she stood and looked around the room for something to protect herself with while Babe also stood and put her hand on Carmen's arm, which Carmen shook off.

"What is this?" Carmen said.

"It's not what you think."

"What the hell am I supposed to think?" Carmen pointed at the man she knew only as Jake. The man who followed her last night. The man who got into a cab with her last night. The man who left the bar, sold her out to Katzev's men, and nearly got her killed last night. "Stop," she said to him. "Right there. Stop."

"Why?" he said, not stopping. "You're unarmed. You're half my size. You don't tell me what to do, Carmen."

She whirled at Babe McAdoo. "You set me up?"

Babe looked offended. "I did no such thing. He's here to help you."

"Help me? He nearly got me killed last night. He sent them directly to me. You know that."

"I had no choice," he said.

"You had every choice," Carmen said.

"No, I didn't. I left that note for a reason. It was to give you a heads up. Don't be naive. They were following me. They saw us on the street. Because of traffic, we lost them at a light when we were driving around the city, but that didn't stop them from texting me. When we arrived at the bar, I waited for you to make your phone call before checking the text. They ordered me to call them, so I did. They threatened me to tell me where we were, so I told them. You would have done the same thing. All we have is our own survival, Carmen. You of all people know that. At least I tipped you off before getting the hell out of there. I didn't have to, but I did."

"So, now you're a fugitive to them?"

"I am."

"Right." Again, she looked at Babe. "Why are you doing this? I don't trust him. Unless you're with him, you shouldn't either. If anything happens to me, you know Spocatti will take both of you out."

Babe McAdoo lifted her pale yellow caftan at her sides and let the fabric flutter against her slender body. "While I love the drama you're creating, Carmen, it's all for not, so just snuff it. Spocatti will do nothing of the sort. You're overreacting. Just be quiet and listen. I'm telling you, it's not what you think." She looked over at Max. "Bring me the phone, please."

Max took the phone off the table behind him and brought it to her. Babe dialed then handed Carmen the phone. "Go on," she said. "Take it before he answers."

"Before who answers?"

"Spocatti. We're here to help you. He'll tell you that. He knows all of us are in this room. You're misinterpreting the situation. He'll make that clear to you, then we can get on with it."

It was a moment before Spocatti came on the line, and when he did he sounded out of breath. "Yes," he said.

"It's Carmen. Are you all right? You sound winded."

"You'll need to ask her if I'm all right, Carmen. Would you like to speak to her? She's lovely. All sweaty and naked and lovely. I know you've always wondered how it would be with me, so here's your chance. She'll tell you if I'm all right—if I'm better than all right—but you'll need to rely on your Italian because her English is shaky at best. Not that it matters much with her mouth so full. Have I told you that I love Capri?"

"Vincent—"

"Oh, and if you're calling about the situation you're in right now, you're fine. Babe's the best. Just listen to her. Trust her. I've known her for more than twenty years and she's as legit as they come. I was debriefed before you got there because they knew you'd have questions and concerns. Lay them to rest. I've worked with Jake, whose real name you'll find out soon enough. Jake is better. You'll see why he chose it over the name his parents saddled him with. Not unlike you, he's being pressured by the syndicate. He did try to help you last night, but they got to him before he could do much of anything. Don't blame him. We always choose ourselves first, no matter what. You're no different. If you were in his shoes, you would have done the same thing. So, join forces with him. Listen to Babe. Find Katzev. Apparently, he is the one you're seeking, from what Jake tells me. And Babe. Now, I'd love to talk to more, but...I can't remember her name...is as red as a beet and wants a moment to breathe. Keep in touch. You know I'm here if you need me. So, I expect to hear from you. Soon."

The line went dead.

She clicked off the phone and handed it to Babe, who gave it to Max, who walked across the room with it and placed it in its cradle. Vincent never would set her up. She knew that. She trusted him as if he were her brother. She looked at Babe and then at Jake, who were looking at her as if they didn't know how she would react.

She trusted no one easily. But she had to listen to Vincent. When it came to her, he'd never be responsible for holding out the noose that took her life.

She sat down in one of the red chairs.

"Babe, if you have coffee, perhaps all of us could talk?"

"I have my private McAdoo blend," she said.

"I had a feeling you would. I assume it's strong?"

"It'll blow your head off."

"That's not what I want to hear right now, Babe," Carmen said.

CHAPTER TEN

When Max brought a tray with a pot of coffee, cups, saucers, cream, sweeteners, and cookies on it, he placed it on the table between Carmen, Babe, and Jake, and offered to pour.

"I'm fine," Carmen said. "Thank you."

She poured herself a cup, took it black, sipped it, decided she liked it, and chose a short bread sugar cookie from the platter. With the exception of the cheese and cracker she ate earlier, she hadn't eaten today. She bit into it and leveled Jake with a look.

"What's your real name?" she asked.

"Fred."

"So, Jake," she said. "Why don't you fill me in on what you know? Why were Alex and I targeted?"

"You're end-of-cycle," he said.

She knew what that meant, but she wanted to push him to see how much he'd reveal. "And what does that mean?"

"Isn't it obvious? Even before you killed Laurent, they were finished with you. They thought you knew too much and it was time to invest in other people as skilled as you."

"Too much about what?"

"No idea."

"You must have some idea."

"I don't. But they think you know too much about something. Maybe them. Maybe something they did. Maybe something Alex did. Who knows?" He leaned forward and poured himself a cup of coffee. "But now that you've killed Laurent, they also want you dead for murdering their colleague. Maybe even especially because you killed him and dared to challenge them. All of their resources are pointed at you right now, Carmen. They want to send a message to the other agents working for the syndicate. Fuck with them, meet your death."

"How many are on me?"

"Best guess? Another agent recently told me that the syndicate employs about seventeen people. Give or take. Probably more. Before Alex died, that included you, Alex, me, and the two men who died last night—the one whose chest I crushed, and the one hit by the truck. With us out of the picture, that would leave about a dozen or so. That said, no one knows for sure."

"Why are you out of the picture, Jake?"

"End-of-cycle. They're cleaning house. Apparently, I also know too much, though I'm not sure about what and I don't have time to find out. I want out of this city and this life. Time for a change."

"Here's what doesn't make sense to me," she said. "If the syndicate wants you dead, why did you agree to work for them last night? Why were they on the phone texting you about my whereabouts?"

She looked at Babe, who was looking at Jake with a furrowed brow.

"Am I the only one who finds that odd? Do you, Babe?"

"I do."

"So, why don't you explain, Jake? How are you a target one day, then their champion the next?"

"I'm hardly their champion, Carmen, but I'll tell you how it went down. The two men hired to kill me last night proved that the syndicate wants me dead. I needed to buy time and figure out a way to get out of the city safely. Because of what you did to Laurent, I thought I had another shot with them and took it. After the guy who chased me became roadkill, I contacted Katzev and promised I could deliver you to him. I told him I knew he wanted me dead, but to give me a chance to prove my loyalty to them. So, I used my contacts. I found you. I bought time. When you left me at the bar alone, I answered their text, left you a note, and got the hell out of there before they arrived. You and I both know that when you're targeted for elimination, that's it with them. Sure, I found you for them. But they'll still try to kill me."

"So, in other words, you set me up for nothing."

He studied her over his coffee. "No, in other words, I bought myself time. You've been around long enough to know this isn't personal, Carmen. You also know I owe you nothing. My first responsibility is to myself. Same goes for you. If I can buy myself time to figure out a way to get out of this city and away from Katzev and the rest of them, that's what I plan to do."

"And yet here you sit," she said. "Why?"

Babe McAdoo turned in her chair and looked at Carmen with delight on her face. "Finally," she said. "The best part."

"What's the best part, Babe?"

"We're going to have an adventure," she said. "My biggest and most aggressive one yet."

Carmen saw it and waited for it.

"It'll be fun," Babe said. "Just the three of us, with Spocatti a phone call away to offer guidance should we need it. Oh, and so long as we call him with daily updates to feed whatever part of him needs to be fed in order to keep him alive, Gelling has promised us access to his contacts. And of course we have mine, which dig deeper into the roots of New York than Katzev ever could imagine. This isn't, after all, my first time at the rodeo."

Carmen held Babe's gaze and sat unmoving. She looked at that weird little Zen bird sitting before her—her red hair and yellow caftan clashing against this room she had sheathed in gold—and couldn't help feeling her gut sink. *Go on*, she thought. *Just say it.*

"Don't you see?" Babe McAdoo said. "Gird your loins, Carmen. We're going to take down the syndicate."

Chapter Eleven

While Carmen met with Babe McAdoo, Illarion Katzev prepared to address the syndicate.

On the massive stainless steel wall before him were thirteen flat screen monitors. In the center, one was left dark out of respect for Jean-Georges Laurent, whose face was blown off at the Four Seasons several weeks ago in ways that demanded a closed casket at his funeral, where people clucked their tongues in pity not because he was dead, but, some felt, because they were cheated out of seeing the ruined nature of what rested within.

The other twelve monitors, on the other hand, were alive with images of unhappy people from around the world, all locked in their safe rooms and transmitting across secure lines.

In the wake of Laurent's death, these people comprised what was left of the syndicate—three women and nine men. None was pleased to be here now, though at least they understood the importance of why they were asked to leave behind their heady lives to deal with a potentially dangerous situation before it became too late to do so.

For Illarion Katzev, that understanding would make the meeting more productive and, when decisions were made, easier to deal with when plans were put into motion.

In the wake of Carmen Gragera's escape from the Waldorf Astoria the night before, Katzev decided to call the meeting in an effort to get in front of the situation before Carmen got in front of it herself.

Each person who looked back at him now knew the extent of Gragera's skills, which were impressive. She wasn't somebody they took lightly—some feared her—which is one of the few reasons they marked her for death several weeks ago, thinking it was time to destroy her connection with them and sow fresh talent elsewhere.

But what concerned them most was her romantic relationship with Alex Williams, whom they also considered a threat because a respected third party informed them that, for whatever reason, Williams had been gathering intelligence on them.

In Bora Bora, they successfully killed Williams, but Carmen escaped, which all agreed left them in danger because Alex likely shared his intelligence with her. And if he had, with enough investigative work, that knowledge could lead her straight to them, which was a concern because with her lover dead due to them, all believed she'd seek revenge soon.

So, Illarion Katzev, a formidable man not yet fifty who made his fortune the old-fashioned way—through murder and with ruthless calculation—read over his notes a final time while the others prepared themselves for his recommendation on how best to handle the elusive Gragera now.

"Colleagues," he said, glancing up at the monitors.

"Katzev," came a dozen replies.

"Since last night, I've been reading over our files on Carmen Gragera and our seven-year history with her. There's no question that she must go, as many of us agreed upon weeks ago due to the potential threat she invites via her relationship with Alex Williams. The good news is that, in researching the information we've compiled on her over the years, I've found a possible Achilles heel."

He let a beat of silence pass and watched the impatience on some of their faces turn to interest. "Carmen loves children," he said. "I have no idea why, since I can't stand them myself. But Carmen loves them in ways that are almost...unnatural."

"How do you know this?"

The question came from Conrad Bates, who owned more of Las Vegas than he probably should, given the financial straits that city was in. Still, for balance, his portfolio offered a wealth of other properties, mostly hotels located in Manhattan, Chicago, Boston, Los Angeles, and throughout Europe, with particular attention paid to London and Paris, where his businesses thrived.

He was younger than Katzev, a product of one of the better Boston families who took his sizable inheritance and actually did something with it. He was aggressive and unethical, which were fine traits the syndicate embraced, though Katzev had never liked the man, not that his feelings for him mattered much. What mattered was the money Bates brought to the syndicate, which like everyone else here, was substantial. It also was critical to achieving what each desired as they moved forward not just into greater wealth, but into what they really wanted— unfathomable power.

"Hello, Conrad," he said.

"Illarion."

"How's Vegas treating you these days?"

"I'm hoping we can address that at our next meeting."

"I'll bet."

"But if you could answer my question now, I think we'd all agree that's more pressing. Or at least it seems to be given the urgency of this meeting."

"In reading over Carmen's files, one thing became clear. Each time she was assigned a job that involved killing a child, she turned it down flat. She gave no reason why. She simply refused to do it. In her files, there are seventeen instances of her doing so over our time with her."

"Who cares?" Bates said. "So, she likes kids. Some of us do. What's your point?"

Katzev kept his features neutral even though he wanted to call the man an idiot for not having the imagination to see something so obvious. "If Carmen loves children so much, then we threaten her with them."

"Does she have children?"

This time, it was the eighty-year-old Greek shipping heiress Hera Hallas who asked the question. Katzev looked up at the elegant woman with the tan skin and the chic, pure white hair pulled away from her face in a blunt ponytail and knew again that in her youth, she must have been a great beauty.

"She doesn't have children," he said.

"If she loves them so much, why not?"

"Caring for a child while gunning down adults is probably a lot to handle," Conrad Bates said.

"I'd imagine changing diapers and changing gun magazines would be a challenge for any single mother. But I still don't see the significance, Illarion. So what if she loves children?"

Patience, he told himself. *Patience.*

"In going through the intelligence, what also came to the fore is that she gives to only one charity."

"Crying Toddlers Anonymous?" Bates said. "Early Onset Childhood Dementia? The Skinned Knees Institute of Montana? The Boogieman Fund?"

Hera Hallas rolled her eyes in reaction to the juvenile comments. In the monitor next to her, another member of the syndicate, who was in Paris, where it was evening, was wearing black tie and starting to look annoyed. Katzev saw him check his watch. Since they all could see each other, he wondered if Bates also caught the man's impatience.

"Actually, Conrad," Katzev said, "regardless of the disrespect you bring to the table, not to mention your cynicism, which is unwarranted, you're not that far off as the charity does have to do with children. Under Franco's leadership, Carmen Gragera's father became an unintended adopted orphan."

"What the hell does that mean?" Bates asked.

"If you pay attention to the news—and I hope that you do, Conrad, beyond the truncated information wedged into the CNN crawl—you'll remember the scandal that broke out in Spain in 1989, when it was revealed that three hundred thousand babies were stolen after their mothers gave birth to them. Does anyone remember that?"

"I do," Hera Hallas said. "It was awful."

"The mothers—often young and unmarried and thus considered worthless under Franco's regime— were told that their child was stillborn. Or that it died soon after birth. When the mother asked to see the child, she was shown, at a distance, a baby's corpse the hospital kept in a freezer. Why? Because her child already had been sold by the Catholic Church. That adopting couple who paid for the child was generally affluent and a member of the church, and thus deemed more suitable to raise the child than a single mother considered a disgrace to Franco and naturally to the church. Franco died in 1975. The church continued this practice for another fourteen years, only stopping when the scandal came to light because a man on his deathbed revealed the truth to his son that he bought him for two hundred thousand pesetas. Or about fifteen hundred dollars. It became a sensation. Worldwide news. Another bullet to the heart of the Catholic Church. Certainly, you heard of it, Conrad."

Bates hesitated, but then said of course he had.

Bullshit, thought Katzev. But he pressed on. "For Carmen's father, the problem went beyond the mere kidnapping. The parents who bought and raised him were Christian zealots. Monsters. They bought him with the sole intent to abuse him, thinking that if they beat this child born to a woman they considered a whore, then certainly they'd be rewarded for their efforts when their time came to enter Heaven's gates." He waved his hand. "Or something like that. They were horrific to him. They did unspeakable things to him. It wasn't until Nerón Gragera was sixteen that he managed to free himself by stabbing them to death while they slept. He disappeared for years. No one knew where he went. It was during that time that he fell in with the right people—at least as far as he was concerned—and was trained to become an assassin."

"So, the fruit doesn't fall far from the tree," Bates said. "Fantastic. But what does this have to do with why we're here now?"

"Carmen Gragera is a wealthy woman," Katzev said. "She and her father were close. It's no coincidence that a great deal of her money goes to one particular orphanage in Madrid and also to St. Vincent's Services' seven group homes in Queens and Staten Island. Each caters to troubled children, all emotionally scarred. She gives millions each year to make certain each organization gives its charges the best care, from living quarters to schools to access to doctors, including psychiatrists trained to deal specifically with troubled children and teens.

When she can, she visits the children. She has grown attached to many of them, especially those here in New York because here is where Carmen often finds herself. I think she gives so much because she wants to honor what her father endured. She took his experience, dipped deep into her own money, and is actively supporting two organizations that need her to succeed. I think Carmen takes care of these children because she knows that by doing so, they will be properly cared for and won't suffer her father's fate."

"How did you find this out?" Hera Hallas said.

"There's nothing I can't find out, Hera. If you read between the lines, much of it is here in the files. Some of it is investigative work I did on my part. With it, I started to piece everything together. Whatever I couldn't fill in on my own was a few phone calls away."

"But to what end?" Bates asked.

"Can't you figure it out?" The person who spoke was the Parisian, Marius Aubert. Katzev looked up at him and saw that he was looking down at Bates, his impatience with the man as high as the tension in the room. "Obviously, Illarion plans to target one of the organizations. I'm assuming St. Vincent's because of its close proximity to him and because Carmen is now in New York. He'll threaten Carmen with those children. He'll tell her that if she doesn't come in, he'll kill them one-by-one until she does." Aubert's eyes lifted to Katzev's. "Am I right, Illarion? Is that what you plan to do? Exchange their lives for hers?"

"Something like that, Marius."

"And then what?" Hera Hallas said. "I'm no angel," the octogenarian said. "But killing innocent children, especially in the numbers you're talking about, seems extreme, cruel, and unnecessary."

"It won't come to that," Katzev said.

"How do you know?"

"Because I know Carmen, and she knows me. She knows I'll go through with it if she forces my hand. She won't second-guess it. She knows I'll even set fire to one or more of those group homes if that's what it takes to bring her in. I expect to hear from her. She'll do what she has to do to protect those children."

"Will she risk her own life?" Hera Hallas said.

"I think she will."

"Carmen Gragera is not without her own army of contacts," Hallas said. "Tip her off, and she'll have those homes surrounded."

"Let her."

"You're being awfully glib, Illarion. How do you propose to pull this off?"

"Just watch me," he said.

"I'd rather hear your plan, not what Marius thinks you'll do. I think we'd all like to hear it."

He knew this was coming and so he told them his plan. He watched the faces first shift into skepticism; he saw them think it through; and then he watched their eyes meet his with what looked like a trace of either admiration or respect. He decided he'd take either.

"Any questions?" he asked.

The room went silent.

Katzev looked over at Conrad Bates, who was staring back at him. He cocked his head at him and waited for a sarcastic reply, but when he realized that even Bates had nothing to say, he knew his instincts were correct and that if he was going to succeed, he needed to act fast.

CHAPTER TWELVE

Illarion Katzev, born Iver Kester in Aberdeen, Scotland, before he assumed the identity of a Russian for the sake of secrecy within the syndicate he helped to create with Jean-George Laurent, had homes in Aberdeen, Moscow, and Manhattan.

It was only in Aberdeen, where friends and family knew him as the boy who came from modest means and a broken home shattered by an alcoholic father, that he went by his real name. In his hometown, he was celebrated as a successful entrepreneur in the States and an example of what could be achieved through risk, luck, and hard work.

With his father long since dead, but with his mother, still alive and thriving in her seventies, he visited his hometown once each year, generally for a week, whereupon he was feted by his mother, his old friends, his aunts, uncles, and cousins. They knew him only as Iver, who left Aberdeen when he was twenty to go to America, where he worked long hours to carve out a fortune in buying and selling real estate, while much of his family remained in Aberdeen to work on the family farm.

What his family and friends didn't know was the secret life he led.

They didn't know that he went by Illarion Katzev, they didn't know that he spent years with a tutor to become fluent in Russian; and they also didn't know that he had spent the same amount of years with the same tutor to perfect how a Russian accent would sound when spoken in English.

There was more.

They didn't know that he owned a home in Moscow to galvanize the belief that he was, in fact, Russian. They knew about the apartment in Manhattan, but because they couldn't afford to visit him, they had no idea that the apartment was a lavish penthouse on Fifth Avenue. They knew he had done well, but they'd never suspect that he had amassed a net worth of millions. And they certainly didn't know about the syndicate, which grew those millions exponentially.

To him, he always would be their Iver, who worked hard when he was young at any random job he could find in Aberdeen, all in an effort to buy a one-way ticket to America, where he was determined to change the course of his life in Manhattan. He succeeded, only in ways they'd never know or understand.

Now, in his penthouse, Illarion returned from his office on Madison, where he had addressed the syndicate that agreed to his plan to root out Carmen Gragera and have her assassinated. In his living room, which overlooked Central Park, he fixed himself a Scotch and soda, and thought through his plan.

St. Vincent's Services is where Carmen chose to give a significant chunk of her money. He learned that St. Vincent's served more than seventy adolescents who directly benefitted from Carmen's generosity. Earlier, he called St. Vincent's and spoke to a woman about making a donation. "I want to make sure that this is where my friend, Carmen Gragera, makes donations. We were talking about it at dinner the other night. I'm fairly certain she said St. Vincent's."

The woman brightened at the sound of Carmen's name. She said that they had a close relationship with her and that she was instrumental in the lives of many of their charges.

"We know Carmen well," the woman said. "She's an angel, that one. She treats the children, regardless of their age or what they might have done in their pasts, with respect and kindness. I can't tell you how many lives she's changed. We'd be so grateful for your support."

"Is there any child in particular that Carmen has *adopted* as her own?" Katzev asked.

"That's easy," the woman said. "There are three. All young women, who at this point in their lives, are probably too old for adoption. Two are fifteen, the other one is on the cusp of seventeen. They'll likely be with us until they graduate high school, which won't be long now. Carmen writes to them monthly and she visits them when she can. I think she sees elements of herself in them, especially Chloe, whom she's closest to. I know she thinks she can help them just by being close to them and offering advice about how best to go forward with their lives."

"And who better than Carmen for that?" he said without a trace of sarcasm, though within, he wanted to laugh at the absurdity of it. "What are the names of the other two girls?" he asked.

"First names?"

"Sure."

Giving out first names didn't rub against the rules of confidentiality set forth by St. Vincent's board of directors. She gave him the names, which he wrote down.

"They think of her as their sister," the woman said. "Maybe even as close as a surrogate mother as they're going to get. Whatever you can do for them and for the rest of our charges would be very much appreciated. I'm not ashamed to say that we rely on any sort of generosity."

"You have my complete support," Katzev said. "But I'd like to make my pledge a surprise to Carmen. Can we keep this between us for now?"

"Of course! I'd love to surprise her."

"That's what I was hoping. I know she'll be thrilled. Are the girls doing well in high school?"

"All three are excelling."

"That's terrific. I'm sure Carmen's influence has helped. But schools are so important when college is likely the next step. Which schools are they attending? I might be able to get them into a private."

"They all attend the same school and it's one of the best."

"Which one is that?"

"Forest Hills? Right near Rego Park in Queens?"

"That is a good school," he said, writing it down.

"And difficult to get in to, but Carmen handled that for us. Carmen worked her magic. They should be getting out soon for the day. Would you like to come here and meet them?"

"I can't today," Illarion Katzev said. "But I definitely will visit soon."

BOOK TWO

CHAPTER THIRTEEN

The following morning, Carmen awoke on a set of towels that smelled so strongly of bleach, she was surprised they hadn't asphyxiated her during the night.

With the shades drawn, her room at the hotel was muted gray, but it was so bright along the periphery of the blinds covering the windows, she could see the sun shined outside.

She swung her legs over the side of the bed, looked around. In the chair across from her were the bags of clothes she dropped off when she returned yesterday evening after shopping for clothes and toiletries in the stores near the hotel. Thanks to Babe McAdoo's courier, on the desk at the end of the bed was a new MacBook Air. The hotel actually had Wi-

Fi, which Carmen considered as close to a miracle as she ever would come to a miracle in her lifetime, so now she was once again fully connected to the world, which was critical.

She reached for the phone on the table beside her and pressed the button for the front desk. "I'd like a pot of coffee, please."

"Here at the Holiday Inn Express, we have a complimentary breakfast that includes Gourmet Folgers Gourmet coffee, which is being served right now in our dining area."

"Folgers Gourmet? Isn't that an oxymoron?"

"An oxy—?"

"Moron. Those two words have no business being together in the same sentence."

"But that's what it says on the can. *Folgers Gourmet.* I've seen it myself."

"And you didn't question it?"

"What's to question?"

"How about just delivering a pot?"

"You can have a fresh cup of coffee and so much more in our dining suite."

"So, now it's a suite?"

"Excuse me?"

"A moment ago, you called it a *dining area.*"

"It's a large serving area, currently thriving with hungry customers."

"Can you please just deliver me a pot of coffee?"

"While we don't provide room service, our documented three-star service nevertheless abounds in our dining—"

Carmen hung up the phone and put her face in her hands. She rubbed it in an effort to wake up. She had to eat. She knew it. It had been two days since she'd had anything of substance.

But there was no way she was eating at this dump.

She went over to the windows facing the street, parted the curtains, winced at the bright light and saw a few restaurants across the way. Each looked reasonably busy, which was promising. She was meeting Babe and Jake later at Babe's house on Park, but she had time for a quick shower and breakfast. She pulled out a pair of jeans, a bra, panties, and a sweater from one of the bags, ripped off the tags, placed the clothes on top of the towels, grabbed her Glock from the bedside table, checked the magazine, placed the gun on the basin next to the shower, turned on the water, and stepped into it. Surprisingly, the water pressure was strong and hot. *Score one for the Express*, she thought.

She was drying her hair with the hotel's underwhelming mini-hairdryer when her cell rang. She clicked off the dryer, went into the other room, and picked up the phone on the desk to see who was calling.

She felt a start when she saw that it was Katzev.

She debated on whether to answer. Instinct and experience told her it could go either way if she did answer, so she chose to let him connect with her through voice mail first. Best not to engage him now. If he left a message, he'd let her know why he was calling.

At least on some level, he will.

She held the device in her hands and waited. It took longer than she anticipated, but finally came the beep signaling a message was left. She put the phone on speaker and listened to it.

"Carmen," he said. "Ignoring me? Really? After all these years? That's a shame. Here's another. I know how much you were hoping to attend Chloe's high school graduation next year, but that won't happen for one of two reasons. You're either going to give yourself up so she can enjoy her graduation and thus live out the rest of her life, or I plan to kill her if you don't come in. Of course, there's a chance you might not come in, that you'll just sacrifice her because you really are as cold as I think you are, so here's the big picture. St. Vincent's, where I've learned you give a great deal of money and support, has seven group homes around Queens and Staten Island. If you don't come in, we will torch those homes late at night, when everyone's asleep, including the other two girls you admire—Valencia and Shenika. Do you understand me? All inside will die. So, be sensible about this. You've lived an exciting life, so why cheat these presumably reformed kids from having a few adventures of their own? Haven't they earned it? I'm hanging up now, but know this—if I don't hear from you soon, you never know what I might do. Or already have done. You know the number. I suggest you call and we'll set up a time for you to come in so we can discuss the reason we're eliminating you. Deep down, you already know the reason. But to be fair, in case you're somehow in the dark about it, we'll tell you in person and give you an opportunity to respond before we act."

The line went dead.

Carmen put down the phone and pulled her damp hair away from her face. She twisted it angrily behind her head, flipped it over into a knot, and pulled it tight.

Those girls meant everything to her. Her contributions supported everyone at St. Vincent's, but for years, those particular three girls had her love, her friendship, and received as much of her time as she could give them. She might not be capable of having children herself, but she had these girls and they were like daughters to her. She'd known them for eight years, she knew their hopes and their dreams, she knew of their rotten pasts, and she'd do whatever she could to protect them.

He mentioned Chloe. Had he already done something to her? If not, he was about to.

She picked up the phone and called Spocatti.

"This is becoming a habit," he said.

"Are you busy?"

"Actually, I'm still in Capri, enjoying the sun. I told Babe I'd help where I can. I have nothing on the books for another week, so I'm available to talk."

"Where are you off to next?"

"Mexico."

"Sorry about that."

"Doesn't matter. All of those unpleasant things I've been asked to do there will buy me a house here, where I've decided I want to live, at least part of the year. Have you been here?"

"Just once." Years ago, her father took her to Capri for a job. She was young, the situation was tense, the job was difficult, but it also was thrilling. When they finished, her father said he wanted to buy her a beer, which turned into five. They went to a small bar tucked away in some random corner of Capri. It was midafternoon, it was mostly empty, and it had only one window that overlooked the street, but her father filled that bar for her with stories about his life that she didn't know, but held onto now. "I don't remember much of it," she said. "It was years ago. I do remember that it was beautiful."

"That's all you remember about Capri?"

"I was there to do a job, Vincent. I wasn't there to sightsee. And I especially wasn't there for a one-night stand." She didn't mention her father. He knew nothing about him.

"Then you don't know how to live. So, what's the problem now?"

She told him.

"That Katzev is a crafty one," he said. "We'll get to him in a minute. First, I'm surprised by you, Carmen. You actually give money to the poor? Who does that? And why are you so enamored by children? Is that the reason you wouldn't kill that little Hispanic bruja on the Wall Street job? The one falling asleep at the kitchen table? The one I eventually had to kill?"

"I don't kill children, Vincent."

"One day, over a bottle of wine in my new villa in Capri, you'll have to tell me why. I mean, come on. They're like whacking a piñata, only money falls out. If I'm asked to target some bumbling six-year-old for execution because his or her parents won't get in line for my client, I'm on it. Quick money. You just sit quietly behind some bushes, watch them totter blindly around a playground like zombies, and when they finally settle down to dig in some dirt like the dogs they are—bam!—they're suddenly bleeding out and creating the sort of mess that children tend to create. Then you're off to the next job."

"It's not for me."

"Your conscience kills me, Carmen, but that's one of the reasons I like you. We all have our limits, though I've yet to find mine. Probably kittens."

"Vincent—"

"So, about Katzev," he said, the joking over. "He'll do what he said he'll do. We both know that. One of your girls will be dead soon if you don't ring him up and offer yourself to him. If you don't, he'll probably target another. And so on until he starts setting buildings on fire. Are you prepared to die for these children?"

"Yes."

"Who is this?" he asked, this time with a note of impatience in his voice. "Carmen? An impostor? Apparently, I don't know you as well as I thought I did."

"You don't."

"All right," he said. "So you want to save humanity from Katzev."

"No. I want to put a bullet through his head for killing Alex, for targeting me, and for threatening those girls and St. Vincent's. By the way," she said, "the irony of St. Vincent's name is staggering, don't you think? Maybe it's your call to action."

"What do you want me to do, Carmen?"

"I need something on him. Maybe his real name, which I could threaten to send to my contact at the NYPD. I'd pay him dearly to investigate Katzev, which would put the syndicate in jeopardy. That's the sort of information I need. Something that will frighten him to the point that he'll back off until I can figure out where he lives and take him out myself."

"We already know where he lives, Carmen."

She was rendered speechless. A rush of questions rose within her, the first of which was why she wasn't told about this earlier. Spocatti spoke before she could reply.

"Babe called Gelling this morning to give him an update on where things stand now. I hear it allowed him to take another breath and for his heart to strike another beat. So, good for Babe. Apparently, Gelling has been working his contacts since you met with him. He's found your Katzev. Babe planned to tell you this afternoon, when you went to her house to strategize. Gelling also has other information, though Babe didn't tell me what it was because I didn't ask. Given the urgency of your current situation, I'd recommend that you contact her now, give her an update on Katzev's telephone message to you, and suggest that you meet immediately so you can get ahead of this before he follows through."

Her phone made an audible click, letting her know a new message had been left. She thanked Vincent, hung up, and listened to the message. It was from Sheila Paige, one of the administrators at St. Vincent's she'd known for years. She sounded on the edge of panic, which was unlike her. As she listened, Carmen understood the woman's panic and why her own stomach sank now. He did it.

He stole Chloe away.

CHAPTER FOURTEEN

Out of all the property Illarion Katzev owned in Manhattan, he owned only two warehouses. The first was unusable because it was filled with items he didn't have space for at either of his hotels or his restaurants, while the second was perfect for his needs now because it contained only his growing collection of high-end new and vintage sports cars.

As such, this warehouse was spacious—none of the cars was parked remotely close to each other. Better yet, there was plenty of room for the other cars Katzev planned to purchase soon, such as the Gullwing Mercedes he was this close to buying.

The ones he owned now simply were here for him when he needed them for a night out on the town or when he just wanted to see them, touch them, sit in them, and be reminded, with surprise, even at this point in his career, that they belonged to him.

He loved them all, these gleaming works of art that shined in the spotlights positioned above of them. As a boy in Aberdeen, when he was just poor Iver Kester, the picked-upon kid who collected car magazines and dared to dream that a better life existed beyond the poverty he'd come to know on the farm but did not accept, he never thought that he'd ever amass a collection such as this.

In the center of the room was something different.

Sitting on a metal chair beneath another spotlight was a young woman with a black hood over her head. Her wrists were cuffed and her hands were in her lap.

Two armed men stood on either side of her. Beyond asking to use the bathroom or for the occasional drink of water from the fountain beside the bathroom, she hadn't spoken since they abducted her late yesterday afternoon when she was leaving Forest Hills High School to return to the group home St. Vincent's provided for her.

Now, she simply sat there with her mouth shut, a gift she probably learned from her days on the streets when keeping quiet sometimes was enough to keep one alive.

Katzev went over to her and, for the first time in several hours, snatched off the hood. The sudden gesture and the blinding light startled her to the point that she reared away from him—not so much in terror, but given the look on her face, also in rage.

He knelt down beside her.

She leaned further away from him, a lock of her shoulder-length blonde hair fell in her face, and she pushed it back over her ear with her cuffed hands. Her bottom lip quivered, but he sensed it wasn't out of fear. Just looking at her now, sensing the heat of hatred coming off of her, he half-expected her to spit on him.

"How are you, Chloe?"

The girl moved to speak, thought better of it, and remained silent. She glanced around the warehouse. Looked at the cars again. Saw the two men on either side of her. Saw their guns. And then, in front of her, she saw something new. A video camera on a tripod. It was pointed at her.

"It's fine," he said to her. "You can talk. You're not dead yet. I'm giving Carmen nine hours to secure your protection. Do you think she will?"

"Why am I here?" she asked.

"Because Carmen loves you," Katzev said. "What's your last name, Chloe?"

"Why?"

"Because I asked you politely and I want to know. You certainly don't want me to be impolite, do you?"

"It's Philips."

"Chloe Philips. Nice ring to it. How old are you, Chloe?"

"Sixteen. Seventeen in two months."

"One day—before you know it, really—there will come a time when saying that soon you'll be another year older in two months will end. That is, of course, assuming that Carmen comes through for you. If she doesn't, you might just top off at sixteen going on seventeen."

"Why are you doing this?"

He behaved as if he didn't hear her question. "Are you from the projects, Chloe? From a poor family? Taken away by the state because you were mistreated? Malnourished? Wound up at St. Vincent's in an effort to turn your life around? Is that your history? Your cheap shoes say it is."

She looked up at him in defiance. "That's about right," she said. "Although you left out the part about my father being a drunk and my mother running off with any man who'd have her, including the last one, who beat me. But, yeah, that's pretty much it. That's me, cheap shoes and all."

"You're a feisty one, aren't you? Is that Carmen's influence or does it come naturally?"

"Carmen taught me to stand up for myself, but when you come from the streets, like I do, you learn how to deal with scumbags like you pretty quickly. Carmen just helped me to hone my craft, if that's what you want to call it."

"Carmen would think you're being reckless right now."

"Maybe. But it's obvious what you're going to do to me, so why should I give a shit? Why not go out with a bang? My life hasn't exactly been wrapped up in some big fucking bow, asshole. It's been shit from the start, so why should it end any differently?"

"I have to say—you are well spoken for someone so young."

"I do well in English."

"That should take you far."

She ignored his sarcasm and looked around the warehouse. "Are all of these your cars?" she asked.

"They are."

"They look like they cost a lot of money."

"They did."

"So, you're overcompensating for a little dick?"

He wanted to reach out and slap her across the face, because he did, in fact, have a small penis. But if he did, he knew that would just send her fury into silence, which he didn't want.

He found himself unexpectedly fascinated by her.

He stood and looked her over. There certainly wasn't much to her. Maybe a bit over five feet tall. Probably one hundred pounds. Pale skin that looked as if it probably turned pink in the summer sun. Pretty blue eyes now narrowed and looking hard at him.

When they followed her yesterday on her walk home from school, there were students in front of her and students behind her, but Chloe Philips walked alone, her back straight, stride determined, mouth set, cheap shoes clicking on the pavement.

When they reached a point that one of his men was able to walk alongside her and ask her to get into the car parked ahead of them or she'd die, she hesitated for a moment, glanced at him, but then offered no resistance when he led her to the curb. It was the most peculiar thing Katzev had seen in years. She simply got in the back of the car, no questions asked.

"Yesterday," he said. "When we picked you up. Why didn't you put up a fight?"

"Why would I?" She nodded toward the man at her left. "Roid Boy here told me he'd kill me. He also had a gun. I could feel it when he pressed his jacket pocket against my back. I would have been a fool to put up a fight, so I did what I was told."

"Were you scared?"

"Are you serious?"

"But you're so calm now. Defiant."

"I didn't sleep last night. Instead, I tried to figure out how this was going to end. And there's only one answer. You're going to kill me. That's what your two brutes are for and that's what that camera is for—to capture it all on film. This is what happens to people like me. It's not going to end well. It never has for me, so why should I give you the satisfaction of seeing me squirm? It's not going to happen. And frankly, at this point in my life, when I've been beaten up in ways you can't imagine judging by your flashy cars, your nice suit, and your expensive shoes, it's not worth it."

"What isn't worth it?"

"Life isn't worth it."

"That isn't true."

"Oh, please. So, now you're going to lecture me on the value of life when you're about to take mine from me? That's classic, man. That's genius."

"I also came from nothing," he said.

"And look what that did for you. It shaped you into the terrific person you are today. Are you proud of how you turned out? Would your parents be proud about what you're about to do? What you've probably already done a hundred times in your life?"

"None of this is personal, Chloe, so stop behaving as if it is."

"Are you fucking kidding me? My life is on the line. It doesn't get more personal than that, dude."

"You're just the lure. That's all."

"Bullshit."

It had been years since anyone stood up to him like this. Usually, when he put someone in her situation, they were filled will pleas, apologies, empty promises, and tears. They begged until they ran out of words. They cried and they shouted and they asked for another chance. But not this one. This one was pissed off, and it came from a place of not caring because of the life she'd been dealt. She confused him and she intrigued him.

He came around and faced her. "We're going to do something, Chloe."

"Really? What's that?"

"You're going to talk directly into that camera. Then I'm going to send the video file to Carmen. Please don't trust my patience and tell her that you're in a warehouse. We'll just end up doing it again and again until you get it right. If you refuse, your friend Roid Boy, as you called him, won't make things pleasant for you. You're a smart girl. Just tell her that you're frightened and that you need her help."

"But I'm not frightened. I told you that. I fully expect to die here."

"Then act frightened."

"This isn't about me," she said. "I'm the lure, remember? You're trying to get to Carmen. Why?"

It hardly mattered if she knew, because in spite of the fact that he admired her spunk, he still was going to kill her because she'd seen his face and could identify him. "Carmen was involved with a man named Alex Williams. Did she tell you about him?"

"She didn't."

"Do you know she's an assassin?"

"That's a lie."

"Actually, it isn't. But she loves you, so try to forgive her. It'll be tough, I know. But you'll manage."

He watched Chloe's face turn to stone. Finally, he touched a nerve.

"Anyway, her lover found out information about my organization and probably told her. So we must get rid of her. We think she now has enough information to compromise us, which is why we targeted each for elimination."

"Who is *we*?"

"The syndicate."

"What's that?"

"A group of people like me."

"There are more people like you?"

"The world is filled with people like me."

"And who are you?"

"Someone who will go to any length to get what he wants."

"When is enough enough?"

"There never is enough. Not for any of us."

"Why?"

"Because that's not how we work. We want it all, regardless of how we go about getting it. We're no better than any government or political leader, so don't judge us."

"Like you did my cheap shoes?"

"Sorry about that."

"Whatever." She paused. "You know, it's kind of pathetic that you justify your actions by comparing yourselves to what likely are corrupt leaders and governments. It's laughable. You've got to see that. The keyword is *corrupt*."

"What I need to see from you right now is a performance. You're going to look into this camera, you're going to put on your 'terrified' face, and you're going to tell Carmen that you've been abducted, that your life has been threatened, and that if she doesn't come in, you'll be murdered."

"You're already going to murder me."

"That's not true."

"Then you think I'm a fool. I love Carmen. She means everything to me. And I highly doubt that she's an assassin. You're full of shit. If there was any reason to live, it would be for her. I won't sell her out. I won't do your video."

"No, actually, you will do it."

"No, actually, I won't do it."

"Sure about that?"

"I'm certain. I'm not going to be part of this. I won't be associated with bringing down a woman who has been there for me more than anybody else. Kill me if you want. As I said, other than Carmen and maybe a couple of friends, I don't have much to live for. I'm reminded of that each time I'm treated like a worthless piece of shit at school, which is pretty much every day. So, just do it. It's not like I haven't thought of taking my own life in the past. What's the difference? Either you do it or I'll eventually do it. So, do it."

"In time," he said. He looked up at the man she called Roid Boy and nodded at him. With one swift move, the butt of the man's gun slammed against

Chloe Philips's temple and knocked her unconscious. Her head slumped toward her chest. Her blonde hair hung in front of her face, concealing it. Katzev studied her critically and decided that the hair had to move so it revealed her face. Looking at her, he felt that they also needed a bit of blood to send home the message that they meant business.

"Hit her in the mouth," he said.

The man who struck her in the temple did so—hard—and a bloody lip revealed itself. From the sheer force of the strike, the blood splattered onto her chin and then dripped onto her gray sweater.

"Get her hair out of her face."

The man did so.

Katzev walked over and positioned Chloe's head so it was tilted just slightly down and to the right. Now, there could be no mistaking who she was when the video was viewed.

He went behind the camera, turned it on, and brought Chloe Philips into focus. Satisfied, he began to speak off camera, delivering to Carmen his own message, which was underscored with the bloody sight of one young woman he knew she loved dearly.

When he finished, they compressed the file and sent it in an encrypted e-mail to Carmen's cell phone.

Chapter Fifteen

Babe McAdoo entered her grand gilded parlor just off the foyer while Carmen, seated across the room in one of the uncomfortable red Victorian chairs, looked at Jake, seated across from her.

No matter how many times she was told that she could trust this man, her gut told her she couldn't. She thought he was duplicitous and, worse, unscrupulous. She didn't want him there. But she knew that if she was going to see this through, she couldn't insult Spocatti or Babe, who urged her to listen to them and trust him.

So, she would watch him. Closely. If he made a wrong move, just one step that gave away his true intentions, assuming he had any, she'd take him out and be vindicated for doing so.

"All right," Babe said, coming around and taking the seat next to Carmen. "We know where Katzev lives. We know that somewhere, he has Chloe Philips, one of the young girls Carmen takes care of through her philanthropy."

"Philanthropy?" Jake said. "That's a bit a stretch."

Babe leveled him with a glance. "In my world, Jake, we call the millions Carmen has given to St Vincent's Services philanthropy. In your world, and with your public education and middle-class background, it's probably called charity. I assure you, with the amount of money Carmen has given over the years, what she's done is nothing but philanthropy. But let's not get hung up on words. We have a situation at hand and we don't have long to figure out how best to resolve it."

She turned to Carmen. "Do you have any idea where he might have taken Chloe?"

"None."

"What do you know about him?"

"Very little. That's how it's always been. The same with Laurent, whom I only met briefly. The syndicate is an enigma to me. It's how they've designed it."

Babe turned to Jake. He was a big man, muscular. Wore jeans, black sweater, black shoes. He was too large for the chair, which likely is why he was leaning forward now because his broad shoulders wouldn't fit easily into the narrow, curving back. His hands were clasped in front of him and Carmen noticed on his right hand that the top of his third finger was bluntly cut off. She hadn't caught that before. She stared at it now and wondered how he lost it.

"And you?" Babe said to him. "Your dealings with the syndicate?"

"Same as Carmen's. You only speak to them via a secure line or through secure e-mail. You're offered a job, the details are spelled out for you, you decide whether you want to take it and then you negotiate the money." He looked over at Carmen. "Whenever she wouldn't kill a child, I usually got the job. So, thanks for the business, Carmen."

"I'm sure you enjoyed the work."

"A life is a life."

"I don't see it that way."

"What would you say to Spocatti?"

"What I've already said to him. I don't kill children. I don't approve of it. There are other ways to handle a situation."

"Anyway," Babe said, determined to stay focused. "Gelling was able to find out where Katzev lives. Or, at least one of the places where he lives. But this is his Manhattan address and the location is so prime and the apartment so large, I'm certain that it's his primary residence in the city. Once, years ago, before I had the good sense to eschew society once and for all, I think I might have even been at a party there."

"Where is it?" Carmen asked.

"He lives in a penthouse on Fifth and Seventy-Seventh Street."

"Way up in the sky," Carmen said. "Presumably, more difficult to reach. But not for me."

"Or for me," Jake said.

Carmen ignored him. If this arrogant son of a bitch got in her way when it came to getting Chloe back, she'd cut off his balls.

"Gelling also did some additional research, which I confirmed through my own contacts," Babe said. "Apparently, his real name is Iver Kester. Hails from Aberdeen, where the majority of his family remains, including his mother, who is in her seventies. Kester has four brothers and one sister, all of whom live within a mile of their mother. They own a farm in Aberdeen. Most of the family works there, including several cousins. Their main source of income comes from the sheep's milk cheese they produce and sell, though none have become wealthy from their efforts. It's sold throughout the UK, even at Harrods, and it does well enough to allow each a modest living, though not a significant one."

"Do we know exactly where they live?"

"We do. But this is what's going to make your day, Carmen. I spoke to Spocatti this morning. A friend of his—a fellow assassin based in London—is now on a plane headed for the airport in Aberdeen. It's a one-hour trip from London, so he should be there shortly. There, he has contacts who will give him the gear he needs should he need to use it. He also will receive various cameras and video equipment. We've asked him to get surveillance photos to us stat. What we need to show Katzev, or Kester, or whatever the hell we're going to call him—"

"Katzev," Carmen said. "Easier."

"Fine," Babe said. "Katzev. We need to show him that we know who he is and where his family lives. If he's so damned secretive about his life and who and what that involves, this information should rattle him to the core, especially since we learned that his family only knows him as Iver. They know nothing about the double life he leads elsewhere, which means they have no idea that their little Iver, who speaks fluent Russian under an assumed Russian name, is really a masquerading murderer turned multimillionaire."

"You have a way with words, Babe," Carmen said.

"I wanted to be a writer."

"Thrillers?"

"Is there another genre?"

Carmen's cell hummed in her pocket, followed by a beep. Someone left her a message. She removed phone and saw it was from Katzev. She stared at it for a moment, secretly worried by what he had to say to her now that he had Chloe, then she told Babe and Jake that it was from him.

"What does it say?" Babe asked.

Carmen opened it. Surprised, she said, "It's a video."

Babe and Jake stood and walked behind her—they'd watch it together. Carmen pressed a button and the video, which opened to a black screen, started to play.

Gradually, Chloe came into view. She was sitting in a chair. Her hands were cuffed and resting awkwardly in her lap. Her head was turned at an unnatural angle. There was blood around her mouth and a bruise just beneath her bottom lip, which looked split. As she looked at Chloe, whom Carmen had known since the girl was eight and considered a daughter, she felt herself start to seize up in fury. Either Chloe was drugged or she was unconscious. Carmen noted the blood on her sweater and knew it was the latter.

Focus. Remove yourself from her. Pay attention to the details.

There was a light shining directly above her, making it difficult for Carmen to get a read on where she might be because everything else was intentionally in shadow. She had no feel for the size of the room, but there was nothing around Chloe. Just her in a chair on a cement floor with a light above her head.

Industrial.

Then came Katzev's voice.

"Carmen," he said off camera in his fake Russian accent, "here is your Chloe. Sad sight, I know, but she wouldn't cooperate, so measures were taken and now she's resting comfortably, I think, until she wakes with what likely is going to be one mother of a headache. I have to say, I see why you're taken with her. She has nerve, which I admire. Did she get it from you? Hard to say since she comes from the streets. Still, she thinks the world of you, which must be gratifying, don't you agree? Even when I told her you are an assassin, she defended you. Refused to believe me. It must feel good to be held in such high esteem. To be unconditionally loved, so much so that Chloe asked me to take her life instead of yours. That kind of devotion to another human being is foreign to me, of course, but I still recognize it as something special and rare."

He let a beat pass. Carmen felt her stomach sink at the news that Chloe now knew who she really was. Babe put a hand on her shoulder. The frame tightened on Chloe's face and this time, Carmen saw another bruise, this one at Chloe's temple. So, they struck her there and knocked her out. The well of revenge rising up within Carmen was growing to the point that she felt like a dangerously fraying thread, something that could snap if any more weight was applied to it.

I want to kill him, she thought, thinking of Alex and now Chloe. *I'm going to kill him.*

"The trouble with Chloe is that 'special' and 'rare' die in eight and a half hours," Katzev said. "That's all the time you have to save her. And saving her is simple. You just need to call me and come in. You'll be given a designated spot to meet. We'll pick you up. Then we'll talk so nothing is unclear to you. You'll know exactly why you're being eliminated, although I know with all the intimate canoodling you did with Alex, you already know. Still, on the off chance that there is any confusion, we'll be clear with you before we kill you. Then, Chloe will be allowed to go free. You have my word on that. So, call me soon. Very soon. As in less than eight-and-a-half-hours soon. I'd hate to have to kill Chloe. Or to light some fires tonight…"

Carmen clicked off the phone. For a moment, nobody said anything. They just processed. Then Babe McAdoo, who as Gelling noted would become more and more exacting and less flighty as the situation unfolded, walked away from Carmen with her hands pressed in front of her, almost as if she was dividing the space before her as she walked through it. Carmen had seen her do this before. This is how she thought.

"We need to think strategically," she said. She motioned toward her butler, Max, who stood beside the parlor's massive marble fireplace, where he awaited instructions from her. Carmen watched her make a circle in the air with her finger and mouth the word *coffee*, and watched him leave the room with a promptness that suggested why they had such a long working relationship.

"Alex must have learned something," Carmen said. "He didn't share it with me, but he must have found out something damaging about the syndicate and they're assuming that because we were lovers, he told me, which isn't true because he knew it would compromise me."

"Any idea what it could be about?" Babe asked.

She shrugged. "He could have had intelligence on them. Maybe he learned who some of them were. Where they lived. I don't know, but it must be something along those lines. Because we were intimate, they're assuming that Alex also shared whatever he had on them with me. *If* he had anything. Regardless, they targeted us both for it."

"How do we go forward?" Jake asked.

"Chloe is my priority," Carmen said. "To get her out of there and to keep her safe, I'm going in. I'm giving myself over to them."

Babe turned her head sharply at her. "You can't be serious?" she said. "No matter what you do, they'll still kill her. She's seen his face. We know how this works. You'll both die there, wherever 'there' is."

"If he gets lucky, he may kill me, but there's no way he's killing her. It won't happen. I'll see to it."

"How can you be certain? They'll strip you of your guns and whatever the hell else you have on you when you meet them. You'll have no way to fight back. We need to explore other options."

"I'm not going to just throw myself to the wolves, Babe. As you suggested, we're going to be strategic." She looked up as Max entered the room with a tray service of coffee. He put it down on the table between the red chairs and she nodded at him. "I'm going to tell you what I have in mind," Carmen said. "I'm open to suggestions, even from you, Jake. When we're on the same page, I'll call Gelling to see if it's something he's capable of doing and also to help him feel connected. If we all agree on what I'm about to propose, I can't have him dropping dead on me now."

* * *

When they finished talking and all agreed upon what needed to be done, Carmen stepped away from Babe and Jake, who were discussing the plan, and called Gelling.

"It's nice to hear your voice, Carmen," he said. "That's my second surprise of the day. The first was when I woke up. I'm always startled by that. It takes me a minute to believe it. The ceiling over my bed is painted bright white and sometimes, if the light hits it just right, as it did this morning, it's blinding to the point that I think I've gone into the light. The second surprise is hearing from you. Do you have any news for me?"

She told him about the video, what she'd discussed with Jake and Babe, the compromises that were made, and the plan that resulted from it.

"It can be done," he said after a moment. "To what extent I'm not sure, but at least partly, which should be enough. How quickly do you need this?"

"As soon as possible."

"It's always as soon as possible, just like it's always Berlin or Beirut, Moscow or Madrid, but never Brisbane. Never Canada. Never Maine."

"We're in a bind, James."

"Let me ask you something, Carmen. You're willing to die for this girl?"

"I am."

"But why would you do such a thing? It's puzzling."

"Because I love her. Because she's involved in this because of her association with me. Everyone has let her down in her life. I know how that feels. He told her what I do for work, so now I'm another disappointment in her life. I plan on repairing that."

"You're a complicated woman, Carmen. Nuanced. You don't think twice about taking an adult's life, but you'll go to great lengths to save this young woman's life."

"That's right."

"And that's why I find you fascinating. I want you to listen to me for a moment. Are you in a place where people can hear you?"

"Yes."

"And it would look odd if you left the room?"

"Yes."

"Then just listen and take from this what you will."

"All right."

"I've done some additional digging."

She didn't know what he was going to say, but the hesitant tone of his voice told her she wasn't going to like it.

"What I found is intriguing. Did Babe McAdoo ever tell you that she knew Katzev?"

"Yes. Briefly."

"Did she tell you that once they were lovers?"

A chill railed up Carmen's spine.

"It was very quick. Just an affair. Matter of weeks, happened years ago and ended badly. But before you go forward with this plan of yours, you need to know everything. It's what I promised Spocatti I'd do. Tell you everything I know as I find out about it. Just before you called, we spoke and he was concerned about the news. Babe and Katzev were lovers and what I've learned during my one hundred and three years of life, Carmen, is that when you've had sexual relations with someone, things become skewed, especially when death is at hand. If she hates him still, it could go well for you. But if some part of her doesn't hate him, if seeing him again evokes a fond memory of a romantic dinner or a good fuck, I'm not sure that she'll go the distance or what that will mean for you if she doesn't. Has she ever told you that they were lovers?"

Carmen looked over at Babe, who was sipping coffee while listening to Jake, who was gesticulating with his hands and saying something Carmen couldn't hear because of the roaring in her ears. "No. Never."

"Shouldn't she have?"

"I would have."

"Be very careful, Carmen. I have to apologize. If I'd known this earlier, I never would have sent you to see Babe McAdoo.

CHAPTER SIXTEEN

L iam Martin, longtime friend and colleague of Vincent Spocatti, with whom he recently joined forces in taking out the wife and family of an English banker who refused to pay the millions he owed one of Spocatti's clients, arrived at Aberdeen Airport with only a carry-on, an overcoat, and a mission.

So the information could be employed as quickly as possible, he was given just over two hours to get the photos and the footage requested of him. Then he'd wire it all to Spocatti, who would send it directly to Carmen.

As quickly as he could, he went to the Alamo car rental agency, where he rented a Lincoln MKX, which would was large enough for his needs, not the least of which was his own size.

Liam Martin, a former Royal Marine, was not only tall but also a former body builder, which had its curses and its blessings. At forty-two and in his line of work, it was rare that he didn't view his size as a blessing. It was only when the situation physically became an issue, such as limiting his possibilities for concealment or fitting into tight spaces, that he wished he were smaller.

Once inside the shiny black Lincoln with its tinted windows, he made a telephone call and simply said to the person who answered, "Fifteen minutes."

He severed the connection, left the airport, and took a left on Dycer Drive. Fall had settled upon Scotland, which now was robbed of much of the deep greens Liam had come to love and associate with it during the several times, often in summer, he had been hired to go there to do a job.

The earth was hardening. Few leaves were on the trees. There was a chill in the air, so he clicked on the heat as well as the heated driver's seat and drove across the curving road until he came to an intersection. He stopped and then turned right onto

A96. He drove for five kilometers before he pulled off on the side of the road, where his contact was waiting for him in a black Audi SUV.

The exchange was swift. Wordless. In a wide leather duffel bag put into the back of the MKX were all the rifles, guns, and ammunition he'd need. In a smaller leather bag were the cameras and video equipment, which were so powerful, Liam Martin could do the work he needed at a comfortable distance without drawing attention to himself until he was given the order to do so. Should, of course, that order come.

He nodded his thanks to his contact, pressed a button that lowered and locked the hatch, and got back into the car to speed down A96. He drove until he came upon B979, slowed, and took a left onto it.

The Kester farm was about sixteen kilometers away. The photos he viewed of it online suggested it was of medium size and used purely for the purpose of harvesting sheep's milk, which they turned into some sort of popular cheese sold around the UK. It was a year-round operation and the sole way the Kester clan made its living. Though the sun was waning, it still was bright enough that he expected to see sheep on the land, and hopefully the Kesters, working with them.

Through Google Earth, he noted stands of trees surrounding the property, which would be perfect for him to hide behind to get his shots, particularly since the property they owned was large enough to require a powerful lens. Even if someone did see him, he'd either have time to get out of there or shoot them should they come after him with a gun for trespassing.

He hoped for the latter. The latter would send the best message, even if it wasn't what he was hired to do.

It wasn't long before he came upon the farm, which he passed so he could have a long look before he pulled off to the side of the road and stopped well beyond it.

His heart hammered with excitement as he turned back. Hundreds of sheep were on the hills. Eight or nine Kesters were tending to them, mostly men. He didn't know who the men were, but Illarion Katzev would. Likely the man's brothers and cousins. Maybe an uncle, since an older man lifted up his hand as he drove past.

But the one older woman he saw in the field. The one with the white hair pulled away from her face. The one who stood on the periphery, calling to the group.

He knew who she was. He was sent her photograph when he took the job.

That was Katzev's mother. And she was out in full view.

CHAPTER SEVENTEEN

In the fog that wouldn't lift, Chloe Philips's mind continued to drift.

In her unconscious state, which revealed to her the blackest of blacks, she heard voices in the haze. Sounds in the darkness. Thoughts of death crept in and she reached out to them, as if the act of embracing them would make them real.

She didn't want to live anymore. She was tired of this life. She hated it as much as it hated her.

As time pressed on (hours, days, weeks), she touched down upon memories she either savored or wanted to erase forever.

Mostly the latter.

She tried to steer around the uglier times and linger on the few good memories her life had provided her, but wherever she landed, in this amorphous landscape from which she couldn't wake, there was no controlling it. Her mind showed her what it wanted her to see, which ran the gamut from the good to the awful.

She was seven. Sunday morning usually meant church, though for some reason that was declining as her mother and her boyfriend now only went when they weren't so "tired." Still, on that Sunday, she woke in her bedroom in Queens and looked across to the other bed, where her younger sister, Mia, was asleep.

"Mia," she said.

Nothing.

"We should get ready for church."

Nothing.

She slipped out of bed and sat beside her sister. The action of the cheap mattress sinking low at its side woke her sister and she looked up at Chloe, her eyes wide and startled. "Is it him?" she asked.

Chloe shook her head. "I told you I wouldn't let him go near you again."

"But what about you?"

"I don't matter."

"Yes, you do, Chloe."

She shrugged. "Come on. We need to get to church."

"Why? We haven't been in a long time."

"It was better when we went. Everything was better then."

Her younger sister, just six but already wiser than she should be because of everything he'd done to them, sat up in bed. "Who's going to wake them up?"

"I was thinking of making them breakfast. Maybe it'll put them in a better mood. Especially him."

"You only know how to make cereal. And you know they don't like noise on Sundays. They yell if there's noise. He'll smack us."

"Then maybe just juice and coffee. I can do that pretty quiet."

"Are you sure?"

No, but she stood anyway. "Go find something nice to wear. Something for church. Wash your face and do your hair pretty. Like I taught you. Use those barrettes we bought at the dollar store last week. The yellow ones that look like bows. Mama's not going to help you get ready for church, but she'll expect you to look nice. "

"If she goes."

"We're going to get them to go. Now, go on. Be quiet down the hallway. Don't shut the bathroom door all the way because it'll squeak if you do. You know how it squeaks. And don't flush the toilet. We'll do that when we wake them up, but we'll have to do it fast so the water is clean when they go to use it. You remember what happened the last time we didn't flush. We don't want him angry. All right? I'm going downstairs. Wear that dress."

"Which dress?"

"Mama's favorite. The pink one Nanny gave you for Christmas."

"I hate that one."

"Mia..."

"OK."

They crept out into the hallway. Mia went into the bathroom and closed the door just to the point before it started to creak. Chloe went down the hall, past the closed door to her mother and boyfriend's bedroom, heard the faint sound of rushing water behind her, and moved down the stairs as quietly as she could in a house that seemed to lend itself to noise and interruption.

The house was a mess, but that was nothing new. What was new is that the couch wasn't empty.

He was sleeping there, breathing so deeply that his snoring seemed to shake the room. She stopped on the second to the last step and stared at him. Her mother gave birth to her when she was sixteen. Now, she was twenty-three and with a man twice her age. Maybe even fifty. Her mother took him in three weeks after her real father left. Not long after, she found this one at a bar and by the weekend, his bags were packed, they were hauled inside, and he was a fixture.

"We need him," her mother told her and her sister the night he moved in. "He's a vet. Got a bit of money and he's not a bad guy. Don't none of you screw this up for us, OK? We need him right now. He gets a monthly check. Now, give Mama a kiss and remember to be nice to him."

That was six months ago and still, she only knew the man as Eddy. Didn't know his last name. Didn't care to ask for it. And if it was offered, she didn't remember it. He was just Eddy, the old man with a violent streak that rivaled her father's.

On the coffee table beside him was a half-empty bottle of Moonshine Clear Corn Whiskey, which he liked to say was "cheap but it sure as shit does the job." Cigarette butts filled the ashtray next to it, along with the stub of a lone, thin cigar, with the crinkly plastic wrap next to it.

Did they have one of their fights last night, or did he just pass out here and she went to bed alone not wanting to drag him up with her? Chloe never knew where they stood in their volatile relationship, but right now she knew he was sleeping deeply and she might be able to pull off this juice and coffee thing if she hurried.

The kitchen was just beyond the living room, where Eddy slept on his pleather sofa as if he was in a coma, and she crept toward it, nearly seizing up when the floor ached beneath her feet in such a way that the wood groaned. She stopped once out of fear that she'd wake him if she continued, but he was so out of it, he was unfazed and kept rattling as if death had rented space in his throat.

She wished it had.

The juice was easy. She put out four short glasses, pulled the carton of Tropicana from the fridge, and filled them. The coffee was more difficult. She'd made it a few times before for them, but right now, she forgot how many scoops he liked. Was it five? Six? How strong did he like it? She couldn't remember. Since a safer bet was smack in the middle, she went with that and started the brew.

The smell of coffee started to fill the humid air. It smelled deep and rich and satisfying, just how they liked it. She removed two mugs from the cupboard, no-brand creamer her mother bought and no-brand sugar, both purchased at the same dollar store where they found Mia's yellow barrettes. She put two spoons next to the mugs and let the coffee maker do its thing.

It gurgled. It spit. She looked down upon it as it dripped. She was thinking that she'd hit a home run, that they might actually come together and go to church today—maybe even have a normal day— when she felt a disturbance in the air behind her.

She didn't turn. Knew it was him. Kept her eyes on the coffee. Drip, drip, drip. She heard him say, "Wake me up for this shit," before he slammed the side of her head with a frying pan and she fell to the floor, unconscious.

"Chloe..."

She heard her name being called, but she was in the in-between. Floating. Turning. Hanging on for the ride. She saw a vision of herself fall when the pan whacked the side of her head, and she wondered how she could see that since she never saw it coming.

Mind tricks.

She didn't see him hit her, but the moment before she blacked out, she did see him standing above her with the frying pan held out at his side. She remembered him yelling at her for waking him up. She remembered him apologizing for striking her later, upon orders from her distraught mother, who had to rush her to the emergency room with Mia, who was in her fancy pink dress from Nanny and who wore the yellow barrettes in her hair.

She remembered her mother lying to the doctors, saying her daughter fell on the pavement outside their house, and in that moment she knew that's how it always would be. Her mother would choose men "with a bit of money" over the welfare of her two daughters every time. And so on that day, with the doctors looking doubtfully at her mother,

Chloe Philips changed her life for a new one—just not necessarily the better one she hoped for.

"That's not true," she said to the doctors. "Her boyfriend hit me with a pan. And it's not the first time he's hit me or my sister. Or done other things."

After much debate and accusations, she and Mia were taken away from their mother that day. Chloe hadn't seen her since. She didn't know if that was true for Mia.

"Chloe. Wake up."

Mia was younger and adopted from St. Vincent's within four months of being accepted into its services. It was done quietly. No one wanted to have a scene with Chloe, who was about to lose her sister, and so when she awoke that morning to find her sister gone, she was told the truth by one of the social workers who worked there.

Mia was adopted into a nice family. The same would happen for Chloe—they knew it would, but things take time for older children, even slightly older children. The important thing is that Mia went into a good home, but before she left, she wrote her sister a note on a piece of plain white paper. Chloe knew her sister didn't know how to write yet and she also knew an adult's handwriting when she saw it, even if they did try to make it look juvenile. *I'll love you forever,* the note read. *Please don't forget me. Love, Mia.*

Chloe tore the note in half and her stay at St. Vincent's began its long stretch into self-imposed isolation, anger, and loneliness. She began first grade in the fall. Her grades were low, but she didn't care. The social workers at St. Vincent's encouraged her to make friends and to try to reach out to others during recess. Maybe music would suit her. Or dance. Chloe ignored their advice and drew inward. Sometimes, she wondered if she made a mistake turning her mother in the way she did. Which was worse? Being in an abusive family, or being here with no family? She wasn't sure of the answer. It upset her that she wasn't sure.

"I'm not asking again, Chloe. Wake up."

It was a year later, one afternoon in September, when she met Carmen.

She was watching television with five of the other kids when Carmen entered the building. Chloe looked over at her and couldn't help but stare. She thought she was seeing a movie star. Or maybe a model. The woman had that kind of presence. Long dark hair that shined as if it caught the light and tossed it back. Black leather pants and a form-fitting white blouse. Beautiful skin, tall and slender, and so, so pretty. For a while, the woman spoke to two of the social workers. Chloe saw her hand them a check, she listened to their gracious gushing, and because the woman obviously knew she was being stared at, she looked over at Chloe and gave her a little wave. Chloe, oddly wanting to meet her, found herself waving back.

"Who is this one?" the woman asked.

The two social workers, both women, followed her into the living area. "This is Chloe," one of them said. She mouthed, but did not say the word, *disturbed*, which Chloe caught, and which the woman furrowed her brow at, as if what they said was insensitive, cruel, and inappropriate, which is it was.

The woman reached out a hand, which Chloe shook. "I'm Carmen," she said.

"I'm Chloe."

"So, I hear. You know, for a fall afternoon, it's a lot warmer than I thought it was going to be when I got dressed this morning. Otherwise, these pants would have been history. I'm having an ice cream at the shop next door. Feel like joining me?"

Chloe, fascinated, nodded.

Carmen addressed the two women. "The ice cream shop next door? I'd like to buy her a cone. Of course, I understand if you need to come along with us."

"Yes, one of us does," one of the social workers said. "It's protocol."

"Of course." She looked at Chloe and rolled her eyes so only Chloe could see. "So, how about a cone? I'm buying."

It was the beginning of their relationship, during which time countless letters, e-mails, and phone calls were exchanged. Carmen visited at least once a month.

As the social workers came to know Carmen and especially her money, protocols slipped. Sometimes, Carmen took Chloe shopping. Or they'd go to a movie. Another time it was just lying on beach towels and sunning themselves in Central Park in bikinis, while listening to dance remixes on the radio. The one constant in their relationship is that they always found time to talk.

Sometimes it was just girl talk. Sometimes it was how Chloe needed to improve her grades at school. Sometimes Carmen would teach her how to deal with bullies. Sometimes they just laughed. As their relationship deepened, Chloe started to feel that even though she'd probably never be officially adopted, Carmen had adopted her. The enthusiasm she showed each time they met in person wasn't faked. Chloe would have picked up on it. She would have smelled the fakeness just as easily as she once smelled the alcohol and pot on her mother and her boyfriend's breaths.

They were friends—good friends—and through that friendship, Chloe started to think that certain things did matter. Receiving better grades was one of them. Carmen was correct. If she wanted a better life when she left here, she needed to go to college. Getting good grades was critical for that, so Chloe started to focus on her studies and her grades improved. As the years passed, she started to allow people into her life, which Carmen urged her to do. She now had two close friends, Valencia and Shenika, who also came to know and love Carmen. Things were better than they used to be. In a year and two months, when she turned eighteen, she knew she could leave this place and step into something better.

And that's what she planned to do.

* * *

It was the slap across her face that jolted her awake.

Startled, she raised her cuffed hands to her cheek and blinked into the light above her, where a shadow of a man's face was inches from her own.

"I told you to wake up," he said. It was the Russian. "You've been down long enough."

Her head hurt. Her cheek stung. She looked at the camera across from her and remembered. They wanted a video of her. Something about her crying out to Carmen for help. When she refused, they cold-cocked her. She must have passed out. Her head and her lips ached. She could taste blood in her mouth. Had they shot the video? If they had, it must have been of her passed out. But since she was unable to say what they wanted, what had they said for her?

Worse, how did they threaten Carmen? And if Carmen hadn't received the video already, she knew that she soon would.

And then she remembered what else they said to her. About Carmen being an assassin. Is that really why she was here? Clearly, they were using her to get to Carmen, but could it be true?

Was Carmen an assassin?

CHAPTER EIGHTEEN

It was the older man who lifted his hand when he past the farm that made Liam Martin rethink his strategy and turn around. The idea came to him quickly, he thought it through quickly, and he acted quickly because he knew that he was right.

He drove back to the farm and pulled the MKX off the B979 and onto a long dirt road that was sided on the right by a weathered wood fence. In front of him, off in the distance, was a large white farmhouse that was likely more than a century old. From a distance, it looked in passable shape. But up close, he could see it was in desperate need of repair. It looked as if years had passed since it was freshly painted. The dark green shutters at the windows were faded, the front port sagged, a window was cracked, and the roof was questionable at best.

Behind it and to the right were seven massive red barns lined in a row, one behind the other, as if they were oversized dominoes laid on their sides and ready to be shoved over, perhaps by a stiff wind. In his rearview mirror, he could see a tornado of dust rising up from the SUV's wheels and announcing his visit. When he slowed midway up the drive and stopped, the dust rolled over the car to the point that for a moment, he couldn't see.

When the air cleared, he looked out his tinted right window and saw hundreds of sheep being herded by several border collies and eight men, one of whom was the man who waved to him when he drove past a moment ago and who looked at him now, along with the others.

Liam Martin stepped out of the car, his friendly face appearing above the hood before his hand went up and waved to the group, who stared in his direction with curious but pleasant expressions.

"Hello," he called. "Is this Kester Farm? Of the cheeses? I didn't see a sign. If this isn't it, I apologize for trespassing."

The older man was closest and came forward with a businesslike smile. He was thin, black hair, pale complexion, eyes rimmed with fatigue but bright with welcome.

Liam knew what he was thinking. They made cheese here. Did they also sell it here? Was this person stopping by to praise them for their cheese? To buy some? Liam was certain this wasn't the first time that someone had stopped by to sing their praises or to buy their cheese. And since it was their livelihood, anyone was a potential customer or already a loyal one. Best to treat them like a friend, particularly with a house in that condition.

"This is Kester Farm," the older man said. He came around the car and shook Liam's hand. "A'm Sholto Kester. Hou ar ye?"

The air stank of manure so badly that Liam was reminded of his own youth, when he was raised by his grandparents on a farm in Witney, where they raised cattle. When he was eighteen, seeing no life for himself on the farm, Liam went into the Marines, emerged as a Royal Marine, and then was recruited for the darker career he enjoyed now.

"I'm fine, thanks," he said. "I'm a friend of Iver's. He told me that if I ever was in Aberdeen, to drive by this way and have a look at where he grew up. We've been friends for a few years now. We did a deal together in New York."

"Whit's yer name?"

"Michael Blake." It had been his alias for years. Not unlike himself, it sounded distinctly British. "So, this is where you make the cheese Iver talks so much about."

"He talks about the cheese?"

"He does." Liam looked around. "Beautiful land."

"Thank ye."

He was aware of the others walking over, including the old woman who wore a pair of jeans, wellies, and the sort of practical layering that wouldn't hinder her work.

He wanted this over with and checked his watch. "I'm catching a plane in a couple of hours to go back to New York, but since you're so close to the airport, I came by between flights to take a photo of the farm to show Iver that I've been here. Do you mind if I take a photo of you all?" He snapped his fingers. "Better yet, would you like to say hello to Iver yourselves? That would be brilliant. I have a small video camera and know that he'd be thrilled. Are you game?"

They all looked at each other and then nodded their agreement. They seemed interested in the prospect of saying hello to Iver, who visited only once each year and who rarely called and never wrote. They started to gather around each other.

Liam went to the rear of the MKX and pressed a button on his key to lift the back gate. Inside the small leather bag were three different video cameras. One was made for professionals; the other two were more pedestrian. He looked for the least intimidating of the lot—a white Flipcam—and came around with it, checking to make sure the battery was charged. It was. Better yet, the camera shot in 1080p.

"Iver rarely comes to visit, you know?"

It was Iver's mother, now standing in the center, who made the statement, her brogue not nearly as thick as Sholto's. He looked at her weathered face and saw that through the farm toughness was a trace of sadness in her eyes at the mention of her son.

"I'm sorry, he doesn't," Liam said. "Maybe this little video will make him feel guilty about that." He smiled at her. "Maybe I can use it to persuade him to get on a plane and come home."

"That would be good," she said. "Been over a year now."

"He won't come," one of the younger men said.

"None of you know that," she said. "Pay attention. I've got something to say to Iver."

That intrigued Liam. He pointed the camera at them, said "Go!" and pressed the red button to record.

None of them smiled for the camera. They just stood there, shoulder-to-shoulder, each weary at the end of a long day's work. Covered in dirt and manure, brown grass and mud stuck to the bottom of their shoes, Iver Kester's family smelled like shit and looked worse.

They peered into the lens as if they were looking straight into Iver's eyes. What Liam Martin saw was a mix of longing to see Iver again, and also anger that it had been so long since he'd visited.

Or, as far as he could tell, given them any financial assistance.

He was about to ask one of them to say something when Iver's mother broke the silence. She stepped forward and held her hands out at her sides.

"You should be here now, Iver. Take this man seriously and come home. Things aren't good here. Things are desperate. We need you now. Not tomorrow. Now. Before it's too late."

CHAPTER NINETEEN

Liam Martin's video of the Kester family was sent directly to Carmen's cell—and only to her cell—via Spocatti, the moment after he received it from Liam and viewed it himself. He attached to it a message: *This should help. Stay in touch. I'll do the same.*

Carmen was sitting in one of the red chairs in Babe McAdoo's gilded parlor and thinking about Babe's love affair with Katzev and what that meant to her in this situation when her phone buzzed and beeped in her pocket. She removed it, clicked it on, viewed the screen. Babe and Jake turned to her in interest.

"It's a message from Vincent," Carmen said. "A video is attached."

Once again, Babe and Jake got behind Carmen and they watched the video together. For the first time, they saw the Kester family and noted how weary they looked. No one in the video was smiling. The way it was shot made it look as if they had been forced to assemble, not gather naturally. One of the men fidgeted. Another stared at the screen in hostility—over what Carmen could only wonder. Still, she was happy to see that nobody here looked as if they were sending home a nice greeting to Iver.

"He met them," Jake said. "I thought he was just going to photograph them from afar so Katzev would know that we had a man there who was ready to take them out if he didn't release Chloe."

"Spocatti chose him," Carmen said, watching. "So, of course, he's good. Let's pay attention."

Next came the money shot, along with the unexpectedly perfect piece of audio that they could use against Katzev: "You should be here now, Iver. Take this man seriously and come home. Things aren't good here. Things are desperate. We need you now. Not tomorrow. Now. Before it's too late."

It appeared as if they were being threatened when that wasn't the case at all. They were just pissed off at Iver, who apparently lived his big life with little thought of assisting them.

"That must be Katzev's mother," Babe said.

Carmen nodded. "Likely."

"How do you want to proceed with this?"

"We send it to Katzev," Carmen said. "We threaten him with it. We tell him that if he doesn't let Chloe go now, we will kill his family and send him a video of that, as well."

"But what if he can't stand his family and would rather see them dead than lose face now?"

"Do you know something we don't, Babe?" Carmen asked.

Babe looked at her in surprise. "What does that mean?"

"It was just so declarative, the way you said it. I'm just wondering if you know something about Katzev that we don't. You did mention meeting him once."

Babe waved a hand. "That was twenty years ago."

Carmen spun her web carefully. "How well did you know him? Was it long enough to give us insight into what he might do when we send him the video or if he even cares about his poor family?"

"Twenty years changes all of us, Carmen. You. Me. Jake. Vincent. We're all different. The person I was twenty years ago has radically evolved. Back then, I was a different person. The same is true for all of us. How can I tell you that the man I knew back then is the same man now when that can't be the case?"

On the surface, it was a fair enough response, but Carmen didn't overlook the fact that Babe still hadn't answered the question. She didn't say how well she knew Katzev. She didn't say she had an affair with him. She chose not to divulge that information.

"I didn't realize that you knew Katzev," Jake said, startling Carmen with the angry tone of his voice. It was clear by his tense expression that he felt he should have known this. That she should have divulged it. And he was right. "How did you meet him?"

Babe shrugged. "Too long ago," she said. "I can't remember."

"Doesn't matter," Jake said. "The fact that you know him certainly should have come up at some point since I've been involved in this. You've never once mentioned knowing him to me. I think it's important that you knew him, regardless of how long ago it was. You know what the man looks like, for Christ's sake, which neither I nor Carmen know."

Carmen looked at Jake differently. He was genuinely angry, as he should be. She watched Babe take to one of the red chairs and sit down. She folded her legs at the knee and was a portrait of calm. "I met him through Jean-Georges," she said.

"Where?"

"Honestly? I don't remember. It probably was at a party. I used to go to a lot of them back them. Several a week. It's something we McAdoos were supposed to do. Go to parties. Attend the right social events. Show up at the right showings. We're part of New York society's old guard, as they say. Before my father died and I became free to do as I pleased, he expected all of his children to follow the rules or be left out of the will. So, we lunched, we brunched, we went to church, we took to the country to hunt, we went to suppers, we spent our summers in Northeast Harbor, we mixed with our own kind here, there, and everywhere."

"Laurent was your own kind?" Jake asked.

Babe laughed. "Hardly. He was an upstart. I can't remember what party I met him at, Jake, but it doesn't matter. He likely was someone's guest at some random event. Same with Katzev. There will always be those with new money who want to be one of us. Those two were no different." She raised her hands in frustration. "But how is this helping our situation now?" she asked. "We need to focus on that video and on Chloe."

"What confuses me is that you've said that you've met him and that you know him. There is a divide there."

"A very small one."

"How well did you know him, Babe?" Carmen pressed.

And Babe McAdoo of the McAdoo family, who was no fool when she knew she was being pressed for a solid reason, as she was now, resigned herself to coming clean. "Well enough to have had an affair with him," she said. "Again, that was twenty years ago. But we did have a little tryst."

Incredulous, Jake looked at Carmen, then turned back to Babe. "A little tryst?"

"That's right. A tryst. It began at that party. I was tipsy. He wasn't. And I have to tell you, he's very good looking. He took me to one of the upstairs bedroom and we had a go of it. Smallest penis I've ever seen—it was like a red berry resting in a nest—but everything else was good. His hands. His tongue. His aggression. We met two times after that, but then I cut him off. He was just using me, and while he had a good build, the sight of him naked from the waist down was revolting. It ended uglier than you could imagine, but who cares? The affair, if you even want to call it that, meant nothing. I should have told you, but I was too embarrassed to bring it up."

"You should have," Carmen said.

"Who told you?" Babe asked. "Somebody did. You pressed for a reason."

"Doesn't matter."

"Probably Gelling," she said. "Gave him another reason to take another breath. Disappointing, really. I thought I could trust him."

"I never said it was Gelling."

"My dear," Babe said, her gaze falling on Carmen. "You didn't have to."

"When did *you* hear?" Jake asked Carmen.

"A moment ago on the phone. I also was surprised."

"Gelling," Babe said. "Dear, sweet Gelling."

"Babe, I hope you see how this information makes us question whether we can trust you," Jake said.

Babe nodded. "Of course, I do. I didn't come clean with it. My mistake. I keep large parts of my life private, as we all do. I, for instance, know practically nothing about you, Jake. You just sit there and judge, but what do we know about you really? Who are you?"

"Just an assassin, Babe. You know how we work."

"I do," she said. "And I get it. I see why you're upset. You can trust me. I'd like nothing more than to see Katzev dead."

"Why?" Carmen asked.

"The reason our little fling ended so quickly? I've never told anyone this, but I suppose I owe you an answer. Katzev beat me. I made the mistake of giggling at how small he was down there. I said it while we were showering after our final romp. I thought he'd have a sense of humor about it because he was so marvelous in every other way, which I told him he was. But it turns out he didn't like that giggle at all. He didn't like me calling it 'Little Willie.'" And because he didn't, he let me have it in such a way that

I warned him that if he ever came near me again, I'd have him killed. We were a lot younger then. He wasn't as powerful as he is now. He was just starting out. But back then, he saw my family as powerful and so well connected that my threat carried real weight. He knew he made a mistake. We were at a hotel when he did it. Some out-of-the-way place on the West Side where I knew I wouldn't run into any of my people. Those things still mattered to me then because Daddy was alive. Katzev gathered his things, left, and I've never heard from him since."

"Is that it?" Carmen asked, knowing the truth when she heard it.

"That's it, Carmen."

"You should have told us," Jake said.

Babe turned and gave him a tolerating look. "When a woman is beaten, Jake, it's not exactly something she wants to relive. I've apologized. I know I should have divulged. I understand if any trust between us has been compromised. Whether we go forward as a team is something for you two to decide. It's simple. Either we're going to work together to bring down that son of a bitch, or you both should leave now and forget that we ever met."

CHAPTER TWENTY

"We send him the video," Carmen said. "Together."

"Carmen—"

"She told the truth, Jake," Carmen interrupted. "I agree she should have come clean earlier—and I'm disappointed that she didn't given the circumstances at hand and her knowledge of how these things work—but the truth is out and I believe her. If you've ever been beaten by a lover, and I doubt if you have given your size, you'd understand the shame that comes with it. You would have recognized that shame in her voice when she spoke about it."

"Are you speaking from experience?" he asked.

"I am."

She looked at Babe. "I'm sorry for what Katzev did to you."

"As I said, that was years ago. I went through it, I learned from it, and I'm over it. Mostly."

"Meaning?"

"Meaning I wouldn't mind watching that bastard take a bullet in the face, just like Laurent."

"Laurent took a few bullets."

"All the better. I could put a spare one between his legs and have a good giggle at the loss of 'Little Willie,' though my aim would have to be immaculate, which it isn't."

Carmen smiled at her. "Mine is."

Babe edged forward in her chair. "So, can we plan this and get it over with? Or am I out?"

"You're not out," Carmen said. "We end this together." She took out her cell and wrote a detailed note to Katzev before pushing the button that e-mailed it to him along with the video.

"What did you write?" Jake asked.

"What Katzev's mother said in that video could be interpreted any number of ways. He'll see it as a cry for help. I told him that if he didn't contact me in an hour with plans on letting Chloe go, his mother and the rest of his family would be dead. I told him that if he contacted them, we would know and they would die immediately."

"You typed more than that."

She nodded. "I also said that if he bothered either of us again, that we know where he lives, his real name, and that the truth about him and the syndicate would be released to the police. Plus, his childhood home would be burned down and that we'd find his family and slaughter them if he tries to hide them. And that, of course, we'd do the same to him." She paused and caught a smile on Babe McAdoo's lips. "Essentially, I told him not to fuck with us."

"It's video against video," Babe said. "Words against words."

"That's right," Carmen said. "So, let's see whose video and whose words carry more weight."

CHAPTER
TWENTY-ONE

In the warehouse surrounded by his car collection, which wasn't there only to look at and to touch but also to remind him how successful he was, Illarion Katzev leaned against his prized three-million-dollar Bugatti Veyron Super Sport Vitesse, watched the video twice, read Carmen's note three times, and then watched the video again.

He was incredulous.

Somehow, Carmen Gragera had tracked down where his family lived. She only ever knew him as a Russian. How did she learn the truth that he was a Scot named Iver Kester from some backwater farm in Aberdeen known for its cheese and that, in the

States, he lived in a penthouse on Fifth Avenue, for which she provided the exact address?

Did Alex tell her this before he was murdered? He must have, which proved that the intelligence they thought Alex had on the syndicate ran as deep as they imagined.

But did it run deeper?

How much did he know about him? The syndicate knew about the security breach, but they weren't exactly sure how much information he came away with because of that breach.

Had he learned the names of the other members of the syndicate and shared them with Carmen? What they did, where they lived? He closed his eyes and willed it not to be true, hoping that the odds were on his side if only because of the stringent safeguards they had long since put into place to protect each member's anonymity via encryption software.

If only because of those precautions, there was a chance that Alex didn't know everything when he died. He may have been on the cusp of learning more, but his death robbed him of that. As slight as it seemed to him now, there still was a chance that his intelligence ended with information about Katzev.

Katzev prayed that was the case because if it wasn't, he knew that Alex would have told Carmen everything.

He lifted his head to the high warehouse ceiling and considered the situation. Certainly, at this point, if she did know more than she wrote to him, she would have used it in an effort to get Chloe back. Or was she holding back, waiting for the right moment to use it for a greater purpose? What he did know is that whether Carmen knew everything or not, the fact that she had tracked down his family and knew so much about him proved she knew enough to be more dangerous than he imagined.

Somehow, he had to take her out. Fast.

There were a few ways he could handle this. He thought them through, knowing that within an hour, if he was going to save his family, he'd need to come through with an answer.

The question is whether he wanted to save his family.

Katzev, who was raised knee-deep in sheep shit by a strong-willed family who broke every child labor law known to man while he was growing up, didn't feel much of anything for them, with the exception of his mother, for whom he felt a tug of something.

Love? He wasn't sure. Did he even know what love was? Wasn't sure. But there was something there. Damned if he knew what it was.

When he went home each year, it was more to see his mother, with whom he had an emotional connection that, he supposed now, upon reflection, might as well be love. As for the rest of them? They could disappear as far as he was concerned. He'd never been close to his brothers or sister, uncles, aunts, or cousins, and while they feted him for his successes in the States when he did go home, he nevertheless sensed a strong undercurrent of jealousy from the men, which is one of the reasons he refused to give them any assistance.

If Katzev wanted to, he could put the Kester cheese in markets all over the world. With a phone call, he could set things into motion that would improve his family's situation. Through his connections, they could be wealthy beyond their wildest dreams.

But he'd never do it.

The only reason they celebrated him when he came home was because he knew that one day, they hoped he'd share his money with them.

It's nothing they'd ever ask him directly—the Kesters were a proud lot and they'd lose everything before they ever sank so low as to ask for a handout—but if Iver ever offered, he knew they'd leap.

He played the video again and watched his mother's face when she spoke. "You should be here now, Iver...Before it's too late."

She looked frail to him. Thinner than he remembered. When he was young, she was strict, but never cruel. She protected him from his father, who could be brutal, if she felt her husband was being too hard on him, which was often. Because of her, he'd been spared many beatings. Should he return the favor and save her and thus the rest of them?

He didn't know the answer.

If he didn't get to Carmen immediately, there was no telling what she'd do with whatever information she had. His mother did mean something to him. He did remember good times with her. He remembered once, when he came home from school with one of his many stellar report cards, that she hugged him and praised him. She often told him she thought he could go far, well beyond the farm, and that he should live his dreams in spite of the farm. She was one of the first to encourage him to reach beyond. He appreciated that, but the syndicate was his and Laurent's child. For years, they built it together and they, along with its members, prospered wildly because of it. So, which was it? Mother or child? What would a mother do?

Save the child.

He looked across the room at Chloe Philips and saw her looking straight back at him. In Carmen's case, what would a mother do? Same thing. Save the child. He knew her skills as well as her vast amount of contacts and he couldn't underestimate them under these circumstances. If she came for him, he knew she'd bring everything she had. And it had become clear that she'd die for this child.

He needed advice, but not from the syndicate. They'd just bicker and complain that they'd been taken away from their lives again and then a cluster fuck of in-fighting would ensue about how best to deal with the situation now.

So, he wouldn't use them. He was, after all, their leader.

He clicked over to his cell and knew that when he dialed the number he was about to dial, it would cost him upward of five millions dollars for the guidance and assistance he needed.

Still, Vincent Spocatti was the best. They understood each other. For years, they'd had a great working relationship. And unlike any other assassin Katzev had worked with, only Spocatti valued money more than anything, including personal relationships, which was critical because Katzev knew Spocatti had worked with Carmen. Would he kill her for him?

Absolutely.

All Katzev had to do was let Spocatti name his price and then wire half the money to his account, which he was prepared to do, and then the other half when the job was done.

He dialed the man's number. A moment passed before Spocatti answered.

"It's Katzev, Vincent."

A beat passed and Spocatti laughed. "What took you so long?"

"What does that mean? You've been waiting for me?"

"Of course, I have. You're screwed without me."

"Why do you think that?"

"There's very little I don't know, Katzev. You know that. I'm fully aware of the situation you're in. When do you need me there?"

"Immediately."

"I figured as much."

"What's that sound I hear?"

"I'm on a plane," Spocatti said. "Just a few hours outside of New York. And here's a tip—until the other airlines catch up, fly Singapore. Wireless. Telephone access. Lovely private cabin to call my own so I can do my work and my life doesn't get held up. Air travel is finally as it should be. I'm assuming you want me to handle Carmen?"

"That's right."

"And what would that involve?"

"Her death."

"What about Jake?"

"We'll take care of him."

"Poor Jake. Ruled unworthy."

"He's a concern, but not like Carmen is."

"Still," Spocatti said. "Just to be brushed off like that. As if he doesn't matter. It's so cold. So...Russian."

Katzev didn't answer. He knew Spocatti knew he was a Scot. He knew he was messing with him and ignored it.

"The price is twenty million," Spocatti said. "Half up front and wired to my accounts at once. Spread the money out unevenly. Once I see it deposited, you can consider me committed to the job."

"Twenty million?"

"That's the price."

"You've never charged me anywhere near that before."

"That's because you and the syndicate have never been in such trouble before, especially against Carmen, who nearly is as good as I am. It's all unraveling, Katzev. Carmen is seeing to it as we speak."

Katzev thought about saying to hell with his mother, letting them murder his family, and bringing in Carmen through Chloe. But he feared he didn't have time. He didn't know what Carmen was planning next, but he knew her well enough to know that she already was planning something and it could be disastrous for him and all involved if he didn't act now. He heard what sounded like ice rattling against glass on the other end of the phone and new that Spocatti was impatiently waiting. "All right," he said. "But we finish it tonight, Vincent."

"Great. That's actually a better fit for my schedule."

"Are you able to contact Carmen? Put her off until you arrive? She's given me a deadline of one hour to respond to her requests, or she kills my family. If it's possible, we'll save them. If it's not, I won't lose sleep over it."

"Such a kind son," Spocatti said. "You're willing to off your mother?"

"I'd prefer not to, but I will."

"So professional of you, Katzev. So removed. I can call Carmen and put her off. She trusts me implicitly, which I've never understood, but she does. She's never understood that our relationship is business and will never be anything but. I'll tell her I'm on a plane to New York and that she should wait for me before she does anything else. I'll tell her I'm coming to help. We'll agree on a neutral place for all of us to meet. You'll bring the girl and only one of your men, no one else. Come armed. That's the agreement. Carmen and I will come together, but we'll also bring no one else. She'll see that as a fair arrangement. In exchange for Chloe, she will promise not to harm your family. Ever. You give her the girl. When we start to leave, when she thinks we're about to go outside and that we'll be safe, I'll shoot them dead. Does that work for you?"

"It does."

"Have a car waiting for me at LaGuardia in three hours." Spocatti gave him the flight number. "We'll discuss any further details later. Oh, and can you do me one little favor?" he asked. "Just the one?"

"What's that?"

"This Russian bullshit of yours is growing old. I want to hear Iver. Can you go back to your sheep roots and give me a taste of Iver Kester, but without the cheese? I want to hear what the real Iver sounds like. The one who is willing to murder his family, especially his mother. It will give me insight into who I'm really dealing with."

Katzev severed the connection and wired the money.

CHAPTER
TWENTY-TWO

In his townhouse on 118 East Sixty-First Street, James Gelling was seated at a desk in his parlor, a telephone at his ear, listening. When there was a break in the conversation, which he considered long-since finished, he said, "Thank you, Bonzie. This time you were helpful. It won't go unnoticed. As soon as I hear anything about either stock, and I expect to hear something soon, I'll be sure to give you a call and share the information before the market opens in exchange for your kindness. No, no. I don't do suppers anymore. I can barely swallow. And I'm in a fucking wheelchair, Bonzie. You know that. I'm one hundred and three years old. These days, I can manage broth and tea, but not always the former if it has too much salt, which causes my throat to seize up. It's hell being me. Good-bye."

He hung up the telephone, wrote a few notes with one of his arthritic hands, and then tried to read what he'd written through the haze of his milky green eyes. The test was simple. If he could read his handwriting, which he could, just barely, then others could.

He had two more telephone calls to make and his job would be complete.

"Frank," he said. "I need Piggy French's telephone number. She has homes in Paris and in New York. I hear she's in New York now. I can't read the damn numbers in my address book anymore, but I know her numbers are there. Would you mind finding her New York number for me?"

"Yes, sir."

Frank, who was so tall, it fascinated Gelling, took Gelling's private book that he kept locked in a safe and fanned through it. "Piggy French, you said?"

"Awful name, but that's what I said. They saddled her with it at Vassar, because when she first arrived at school, she was a bit too fat for that crowd. When she lost the weight in a matter of months and became svelte, she decided to keep the name as a reminder to not gain it back and also not to bow to her bullies. When her transformation was complete, a beautiful girl was revealed. She and her name became chic. The irony! But then everything went to hell for her when she married and divorced and became a drunk of the highest order. This is the sort of useless information I'm filled with."

Frank gave Gelling her number and Gelling, in the meantime, tried to read the time on the watch stitched into Frank's eye patch. Not great, but he did have some time left. "Would you like me to dial it for you?" Frank said.

"That would be helpful, Frank. My fingers are like pretzels. Here. Give me the receiver. At least I can hold it."

Within a few moments, he was speaking to Piggy French.

"Piggy," he said. "It's James Gelling. How are you?"

"Right now, a little drunk, James. Peter left me."

"Sorry about that."

"Probably for the best."

"Was is the drink?"

"Was it the what?"

"What it the drugs?"

"Was it the what?"

"Never mind. I assume—"

"Don't worry. This time, I had an airtight prenup. What's left of Daddy's money is safe. I learned all about *that* after Dick left me."

"Why did Dick leave you again?"

"He called me a cunt at Maisie Van Prout's swank dinner party for that sheik everyone loves. Whatshisname *Quelquechose*. Can't remember right now. But I remember the scene as if it were stamped on vellum. Can you imagine? That language hurled at me in front of the sheik and everyone else at the table, which included the legendary Broadway actress, Eve Darling? When that prick left the room, I excused myself and immediately stuck my nose in some peonies Maisie had arranged in a vase in her living room. I just breathed them in. The scent calms me. So sweet. When he took me to court and got his ten million, I did it again at my own house. Stuck my nose straight in a vase filled with my own peonies. They didn't work as well that time, probably because losing ten million to a bastard like Dick Weatherbee is worse than being called a cunt by him in front of a popular sheik and a Broadway legend who was in the bathroom snorting coke throughout the evening."

She was slurring her words. "What are you drinking, Piggy?"

"Little bit of everything."

"Pills?"

"Not yet."

"Don't do the pills."

"I loved him, Jamesie."

"You'll feel different in a week. You need to focus on that. You need to think, *rebirth*. Get through the week and you'll see things differently."

"A week will feel like a year. A lifetime!"

"No, it won't. And don't get all hysterical on me. I'm too old for it. I need you to do this."

"OK."

"And as long as I'm still here, which could end at any point, as in minutes—seconds!—I'm available if you need to talk."

"OK."

"Thanks, Piggy. I hate to call you when you're so down, but I need some information."

"OK."

"You know I'm discrete."

"It's why I love you. And why I confide in you. Everyone confides in you. Some still think you're still a practicing shrink."

He hated the word *shrink*, but he went with it because she was in no condition to be corrected. "Sometimes, I think I still am. But I'm not, though my ethics have remained when it comes to honoring that profession. My lips are as tight as a priest's, which isn't saying much these days. Let's just say they're tighter."

"You've got a filthy mind and I love you for it. What do you want to know, Jamesie?"

He hated it when she called him *Jamesie*, but now was not the time to ask her to call him *James* or even *Gelling*. He needed information from her, so he just went with it. "You and I both know that you had Dick Weatherbee dealt with. You told me so yourself in one of our many unplanned sessions."

There was a silence. "I don't, uh, remember that. Was I drunk when I told you?"

"Sloshed. You were on the floor of your room at the Ritz Carlton in Paris and called me about an hour after it happened. You said you had crackers, good vodka, and cheap potato chips all around you. You said you were on a binge."

"Jesus."

She said it like, "Hey-Zeus," which surprised him. "Piggy, are you part-Hispanic?"

"No, no. I just love the Romance languages. I use them often."

"Anyway, your secret has and always will be safe with me. But I seem to remember that you mentioned a woman's name in connection with the whole thing. It was Greek. Do you remember her name?"

Piggy said nothing.

"Now's not the time to go all quiet, Piggy."

"OK."

"If I read you the list of names I have in front of me, would you recall the name you used to off Dick?"

"What's this about, Jamesie?"

"It has nothing to do with you. I promise you that. I'm investigating a syndicate, which you mentioned to me that night when you were drunk and eating cheap potato chips at the Ritz. You said they were instrumental in bringing down Dick. I just need her name because I'm being threatened by her through them and I need to have her handled, if she's who I think she is."

"Why are you being threatened? You're an angel."

She said "angel" like "an-hell."

"Piggy, drop the Romance."

"OK. But you *are* an angel."

"Apparently, someone feels otherwise."

"Who do you think it is?"

"I have it narrowed down to three names. I know she belongs to that syndicate. Does the syndicate ring a bell?"

"Right now, bells are clanging all around me, Jamesie. Let's just cut to the chase and quit the guessing games. I want to help. This list of yours. I'm assuming Hera Hallas's name is on it? The Greek shipping heiress? The one I went to for...uh, you know...assistance?"

"She is."

"I don't believe in coincidences, Jamesie. Why are you in trouble?"

"I have no idea, but now I can find out. I can threaten her with exposure. I owe you one, Piggy."

"If it gets bad, this thing with me and Peter, who left me with that cruel look on his face and that hateful barb I refuse to repeat because it's beneath me, I might need to call you a few times. Talk things through. Clear my head. Is that OK?"

"Did he also call you a cunt?"

"He said it four times. Is that what I am, Jamesie? Am I really that? Two men have called me that now. Two men! And then guess what he said? He said that word wasn't even low enough to describe the monster I am."

"You're no monster," he said. "And, yes, call me. Just not when I'm sleeping. At my age, I might be having my final rest, which I'd rather like to enjoy. Call late mornings or afternoons. We'll see if I'm still around. At my age, it could be lights out at any point, Piggy. I could drop dead after this phone call."

"Don't say that."

"It's true."

"I can't bear it."

"You've got to face it sometime."

"Not that."

"And Piggy," he said.

"*Oui?*"

"*Ne prenez pas les comprimés.*"

"What?"

"Don't take the pills."

CHAPTER
TWENTY-THREE

"Frank," Gelling said. "Would you help me find another number? Yes? Sims Cliveden. This will be the last one. No time for others. Sims will know what I need to know because I happen to know he didn't kill his mistress himself, all those years ago, on that awful night in Sagaponack, when it happened by a hand that wasn't his. He's a coward. He hired it out. Guilt brought him here one evening and he told me all about it in such a gushing, blubbering rush, I think he thought I could offer him atonement. All I could do was listen and not judge, which is what I do best. But what I remembered earlier today while thinking about this syndicate angle I'm pursuing was being confused at the time of Sims's breakdown because it was the first time I heard mention of the syndicate, which he talked about. Sims used them. He must have. And it has to be the syndicate we're after. I mean, how many syndicates *are* there?"

He looked at Frank as the man raised an eyebrow and then he held up his frail hand as far as he could lift it, which wasn't far, given the arthritis that had consumed it. "Don't answer. You're a former Marine chock-full of intelligence and it might ruin this for me. Here's the book. You'll find his number in there."

"Would you like me to dial again for you, sir?"

"That would be great, Frank. You know I can't see shit. And I've got pretzels for fingers. Sometimes I'm surprised when I whiz around this joint in my wheelchair that I don't crash into things."

"Sometimes, I worry about that, sir."

"Don't. I know every nook. Every cranny. It's my racing track and it's my escape."

"Here's the number."

"Perfect. You know, Frank, once this is finished, I'll have all of the names of those who comprise the syndicate. Or at least a good deal of those names. There's likely more, but this is a good start and if

Carmen uses the list correctly, which she will, it will rattle the cages. And then we'll see what Illarion Katzev does then. Time is of the essence. Beyond helping her, I think this Katzev person will piss in his kilt when he finds out about the list because he'll know that when it's in Carmen's hands, it's a game-changer."

He saw the confused look that crossed Frank's usually stoic face and explained. "Katzev was born Iver Kester on a second-rate Aberdeen sheep farm before he turned Ruskie, hooked a flight to the States, and started watching too many American mafia movies, the lot of which informed who he is today. He's a Scot through and through, but he'd deny it in a minute. An old acquaintance once told me that he spent years with a personal tutor, who taught him how to speak perfect, fluent Russian, and also how to speak English as if his native language was Russian. Who *thinks* like that? If I was younger and still publishing for the journals, I'd write a case study on him in a second."

He looked up at Frank's bum eye, checked the time on the sapphire-colored watch that gleamed there, then switched to the other eye to be polite.

"This has been invigorating. All this sleuthing. Thank heavens I once treated so many wealthy, murdering swells. It's exciting. You realize, this might have even bought me another year. I can feel my heart beating like a young man's again. Can you read my handwriting here?"

He showed Frank the piece of paper with the list of names, addresses, and other information.

"Yes, I can."

"Everything?"

"Everything."

"Perfect. OK, dial Sims or me. I'll remind him what I know about him and his mistress. He'll talk. Like Piggy French, Sims Cliveden always talks. The good news is that you just don't need him to be drunk or on pills to do so."

* * *

Later, Sims Cliveden of the Pittsburgh Clivedens, told Gelling the name of the person he used to knock off his mistress, Jacqueline, nine years ago, before she came through with her threat of causing trouble between Sims and his wife of twenty-three years, Florette.

Gelling knew the story because at the time of Jacqueline's death, Sims was his client and, guilt-ridden Catholic that he was, he blushed when he told him everything during one of their sessions.

Gelling went to his files and found his old notes. The man Sims used was named Conrad Bates. For some reason, the name sounded familiar to Gelling— he sensed there was a Northeast connection—though he didn't know why and it certainly didn't matter now.

What mattered was that he had compiled eight names, and while he doubted that covered all who belonged to the syndicate, it was plenty to arm Carmen with the information she needed to disarm Katzev now.

He read the list over again and, with pride, he placed it back on the desk. In a moment, he'd call Carmen with the information and have her come pick it up. This was her trump card against Katzev and the syndicate. And he'd made it happen.

Even at my age, he thought with a thrill.

In a whirring rush, he backed away from his desk in his electric wheelchair and looked around the room for Frank, who must have left either to use the bathroom or to grab himself something to eat.

Leave him alone, he thought to himself, a whiff of an idea already forming. *Opportunity knocks.*

Five months after his ninety-sixth birthday, James Gelling was told by doctors that he'd never walk again. His hips, replaced twenty years earlier, had worn out, as had his replaced knees, which now locked whenever he went up or down stairs.

He wanted to undergo surgery to replace his hips and his knees, but due to his age, his doctor warned him against it. "It's unlikely that you'll make it," the woman said. "It's too risky."

"Why?" Gelling asked.

"You know why."

"The gas?" he said.

"That's right," she said. "The gas. And also your age. You're not young anymore, James. The surgery will be too much for your body to handle, especially given the length of it. It will kill you. You know that. Unless I'm misreading you, I don't think you want that to happen."

"You don't know what I want." He paused as a sense of defeat overcame him. He wanted a normal life. He wanted to continue his practice, but she also asked him to end it because he needed his rest. The idea infuriated him. She was taking away everything that mattered to him. "Are you suggesting I spend the rest of my life in a wheelchair until death carries me out of it?" he asked.

"What I'm giving you is my best advice," she said. "And, no, that's not what I'm suggesting. With assistance, you still can have a meaningful life. What you need to figure out is what that life will be in your current situation."

He remembered looking out a window and losing himself in the rainy gray gloom of the Manhattan skyline.

"I've started to shit my pants," he said in a distance voice. "I haven't told you about that. I wear a diaper now, which I can't change myself, so there's the added humiliation that someone has to change it for me and wipe my ass because I've become incontinent. The man who does it is Frank. He's a gem. A great guy, former Marine, taller than is genetically possible, though he has only one eye and I'm dying to see what's beneath the patch. He won't show me. Probably humiliated. Obviously, embarrassed. I know that feeling. What I love about him is that he's an eccentric. He has a watch stitched into the front of his patch. Can you imagine? I think he does it to put people off—they don't know where to look when they address him. I know I'm lucky to have him, but I want to walk again. I don't want to be in a fucking wheelchair."

"Who does?"

"But that's where you're putting me. What am I going to do in a wheelchair? Seriously?"

"Something different. Something that matches skills you don't even know you have. You need to come to terms with this. You've had a good life, James. And with the exception of your legs and your knees and your deformed fingers, you're also in excellent health, which many people half your age can't claim."

"My deformed fingers. Is that also supposed to make me feel better?"

"It's meant to give you a sense of scope. You've had a good ride. You can still enjoy more years, especially if you find a new reason to get up in the morning. A new kind of career."

He consulted other doctors, but to his disappointment, they all agreed. Surgery would be the end of him. He'd die on a table with one of his titanium hips already removed, but instead of putting it back properly inside his corpse, he knew how it worked. They'd just shove it back inside improperly and sew him up, regardless of how bad it looked.

For Gelling, who had very specific plans for his own funeral and burial, to the point that he hired a theatrical agency to plant nine character actresses of various ages along the periphery of his grand mahogany casket, where they would weep for him when he went into the hole, the thought of going into the dirt with such a disfigurement repelled him.

When he finally decided to give himself over to life in a wheelchair, he bought the top-of-the-line turbo model he used now. And then he rethought his life.

What were his passions? What did he want to do before he died? It was when his longtime acquaintance Babe McAdoo called to ask him for a favor, which involved tracking down a man she knew he knew through mutual friends, that he started to suspect things about her that he couldn't have known when the man was found beheaded days later.

It was an event that made international news because of who the man was. Over drinks, which he demanded she share with him, he learned of her "secret life," as she called it, which stunned him, but which he found rife with excitement.

"You know a lot of people," Babe said to him. "More than anyone I know, really, including me, which is saying plenty. And you've always had an inquisitive mind. You're good with puzzles and you understand the human mind in ways that most don't because of your medical background and your longtime practice. You could still be an asset to certain people I know. And you could do it all from that chair."

Before she left, he was sold on the idea. And his life, at ninety-six, began anew with a string of thrilling adventures he never dreamt of having in his townhouse off Park, which had been streamlined and decluttered to accommodate the wheelchair.

When he was feeling good, as he was today because of how he'd helped Carmen, he sometimes zipped around his apartment, as if he were the boy he used to be. What did he have to lose? His body may have failed him years ago, but Gelling's sense of adventure never had left him, even if it was only racing around his townhouse's fourth floor at speeds that Frank often paled at because he worried that the chair might topple over, regardless of the fun Gelling was having.

Gelling sat in his chair and listened to the house. His ears weren't what they used to be, but they weren't bad, and if he were a betting man, which he was, he'd wager that he heard Frank in the kitchen downstairs, probably fixing himself the turkey sandwich he usually had around this time of day.

Knowing that Frank would scold him but not really caring, Gelling looked to his right and saw the long gleaming hallway that led out of the fourth-floor room he'd turned into his second parlor. In his condition, it was more convenient to have another parlor on the fourth floor, where he lived, than on the first floor, where he rarely spent his time.

He listened to the house again, heard nobody on the stairs and then, with a smile, he propelled the wheelchair forward.

The chair was fast and robust. Soon, he was free, racing from room to room, hallway to hallway, at such speeds that he couldn't help a laugh and a gasp. He cut around tables and furniture, nearly toppled over, but somehow righted himself and went forward faster and faster, his usually pale face flushed pink with grinning excitement until the wheelchair malfunctioned.

It all happened so quickly, Gelling wasn't sure what to do as he raced down the long hallway that opened into the parlor, which dead-ended at a large French window that overlooked East Sixty-First Street, just off Park, four stories below.

While trying to steer in a straight line so he wouldn't topple over, Gelling yanked back on the handle, which was stuck in its forward position and thus shooting him forward.

The fourth-floor parlor was a large room, about fifty feet long, but Gelling already was past the halfway mark and he wasn't strong enough at this speed to do anything more than to watch the inevitable bloom before him.

So, this was it. His death wouldn't be natural, as he always thought it would be. He wasn't going to open his eyes one morning and realize that the white ceiling actually was a bright light that opened into another world. He wasn't going to slump over dead in his chair while sipping his soup. He wasn't going to expire from the sheer embarrassment of watching Frank wipe his ass and change his diaper, which he detested and caused him great stress.

Instead, his death ironically was going to end with great disfigurement, just as it might have if his hips and knees had been replaced, as he had wished.

The idea of disfigurement was something he couldn't bear, but with death so close, he knew it was the case. The wheelchair slammed against the bottom of the window, catapulted him through the glass and into the open air, which felt so cold to him, it was as biting as everything now happening to him.

At that moment, when he was airborne, his body so rigid from age that he couldn't lift his hands in front of his face to keep it from directly connecting with the sidewalk, James Gelling shit his pants a final time, a further humiliation met at life's end. He shouted out for Frank, such a gem, whom he was sad he wouldn't see again.

And then it was over.

While people stopped on the sidewalk to shriek or to stand transfixed in horror or to turn away for the same reason, he became an unfortunate part of the pavement, with Carmen's list of names left behind him on his desk.

CHAPTER TWENTY-FOUR

Carmen sat with Babe and Jake in the parlor, occasionally checking her watch, worried beyond worried for Chloe, but trying to keep her emotions in check so she could stay focused and resolve the issue when she had the opportunity to do so.

The hour they'd given Katzev to respond had dwindled by half. There'd been no response from the man who held Chloe captive and whose family's welfare was on the line because of it.

"What's taking him so long?" Babe asked.

"He's playing the game, Babe. He's making us sweat. But he'll call. Just a matter of time."

Five minutes later, the cell phone she held in her lap buzzed. All looked at Carmen, who looked down in surprise to see that it was Spocatti calling.

"It's Vincent," she said. She clicked on the phone and held the receiver to her ear. "This is Carmen."

"So formal," Spocatti said. "This is Vincent."

She could hear the distinct rumblings of a plane. "Where are you?" she asked.

"On my way to New York."

"You're coming here?"

"I'll be there in a few hours."

"What for?"

"To help you. I contacted Katzev. I understand you've given him one hour to offer up this Chloe girl you're so concerned about, but I need you to back off."

"Why?"

"I'm not asking you to back off forever, Carmen. Just until I get there. Then, in exchange for the safety of his family, he's agreed to release Chloe and let her go. Turns out sending Liam there was the right thing to do—Katzev is shaken. He's agreed to meet at a neutral place, still unannounced by him, but which we'll both agree upon soon. He will come with the girl and one of his men. Both Katzev and the other man will be armed. I told him that I would arrive only with you, and that we also would be armed. So, at the very least, when it comes to artillery, we're even."

"If we can trust him, which is a stretch."

"I think we can, but you're right—we'll never know. That said, I heard his voice. He knows you're serious. He especially doesn't want anything to happen to his mother. I don't think he cares much for the others, but his mother does mean something to him. She's the one he wants to protect."

It's what Carmen sensed. "So, Chloe's safe," she said. "What happens to me?"

"That's where things get sketchy."

"How?"

"We'll all be armed, Carmen. The mood will be tense. I don't know what he'll do, but you need to keep your eyes on him throughout the process and be prepared for him to shoot you, because he will if he has the chance. If you sense that he or his man are about to go for their guns, you shoot them. Period. If they don't, we'll back out of there. I'll also be watching him. Together, we can take him out if he tries something stupid, but there are consequences if we do. When they learn of Katzev's death, the syndicate will put all of their resources into tracking us down and killing us. We will be their number-one priority. They won't allow two of their chief members to be murdered by anyone, especially since they're convinced you have dirt on them. It will be war. If it happens, we'll need to seek out each member and end this for good."

"Why are you doing this, Vincent?"

"Doing what?"

"Helping me and Chloe when you yourself will become a target?"

"Because I want to."

"That doesn't sound like you."

"Carmen, you've come to mean something to me. I know the risks. I've made my decision. Would you rather I step out of it?"

"No."

"All right, then."

"I think I might have an edge when it comes to learning who's in the syndicate," Carmen revealed.

"How?"

She thought of her conversation with Gelling. If he pulled through for her with their names, addresses, and whatever else he could find out about them, the balance would shift in her favor. The syndicate either would have to back down or risk death or exposure.

"I'll tell you when you get here. And, Vincent, I have to reiterate, the syndicate is my problem, not yours. I'll take them out. There's no need for you to risk your life for me."

"I don't offer assistance to just anyone, Carmen. Especially for free. Just like you, I've worked with the syndicate for years. They've grown too powerful. They've become arrogant, which is dangerous. I think it's time to end them before they end us, as they started to do with Alex, and now with you and Jake. Who knows? I hardly walk on water. I might be next."

"All right," she said. "But hear me on this. They're responsible for Alex's death. If only for him and also because of what he's done to Chloe, I want the pleasure of taking out Katzev myself."

"He's yours. But we both know that if you go for Katzev, his guard will go after us."

"I don't see that as a problem."

"I do. We don't know how skilled he is. We'll need to act swiftly."

"Call me when you arrive?"

"I will. This ends tonight. By the time I land, Katzev and I will have agreed upon a location. Let Babe and Jake know I'll be coming by to pick you up, and only you. They'll be disappointed, but those are the terms."

"Understood."

"And Carmen," Spocatti said, a new note to his voice.

"Yes?"

"This all could go wrong in ways that neither of us expected or wanted. I want you to know that no matter what happens, I've always admired you."

* * *

Moments later, when Carmen delivered the news that Babe and Jake were out and that she'd be proceeding alone with Spocatti, who was en route to New York as they spoke, Babe's butler Max entered the room with unusual haste and bent down to Babe's ear, where he whispered something Carmen couldn't hear.

Babe looked up at him. Her jaw dropped. "No," she said.

Carmen watched the woman's face go pale.

"I'm afraid so, ma'am."

"But it can't be."

"What's the problem?" Carmen asked.

"It's Gelling," Babe said. "Terrible accident. Just terrible."

"What happened?"

"Somehow, he went through his fourth-story window. People on the sidewalk saw him smash through it."

"What are you talking about? Is he all right?"

She shook her head. "No," she said. "Gelling isn't all right at all. He shot through the window, fell to the sidewalk and now he's dead. Poor Gelling is dead. Max just saw it on CNN."

Carmen sank back in her chair. Beyond the fact that she had grown fond of Gelling, whatever information he'd culled that afternoon on the syndicate had died along with him. It was her one trump card against Katzev, that one thing she knew she could use against him if the situation called for it, which she knew it would.

Sitting there, stunned by the news, she knew that now she only had Katzev's family to use as a bargaining chip against him. But already she knew that wasn't much. What she saw in that video was a family struggling to keep it together. With Katzev's money, why weren't they in a better situation? Had he refused to help them? Obviously, he had. They meant little to him, including his mother, whom he could have set up with a better life if he wanted to do so.

Worse for Carmen, if they did mean nothing to him, would it matter if she threatened to kill them? And if it didn't, what pull did she have over him now?

* * *

"Where are you meeting Katzev tonight?" Jake asked.

"I'm not sure," Carmen said. "Vincent said he'd find out by the time he landed."

"You know you can't go there alone."

"I'm not going there alone. I'm going with Vincent."

"I should be there," he said. "Katzev will have his own people there, wherever 'there' is. It's not going to be just him."

"Probably not, but I can't risk it. At the very least, I need to get Chloe out of there. You don't understand what she means to me. She's like a daughter to me. She's in that situation because of me. Whatever happens to me happens. My main focus is getting her out and following Vincent's plan."

"Even if you die?"

"Even if I die."

He looked at her with disappointment, as if that fact that she'd choose her death to save someone else's life was an affront to his ideals as an assassin. "I'm not exactly an amateur, Carmen. They won't see or hear me. Let me help you."

What Carmen wanted to say but didn't say is that she still didn't trust him. She still didn't know who he was. He was an enigma to her. Since they'd been together, he had shared almost nothing about himself. Who was he? What did she know about this man that was meaningful? Nothing. There had been opportunities for him to offer a glimpse into who he was when they were conferencing with Babe, but he chose to remain behind a shadow of his own making.

Part of her understood that. It's what they were supposed to do—keep quiet. Reveal nothing. He was honoring his profession. She got it. But she would feel a hell of a lot better if she knew something real about him.

She looked at him. He said he had no idea why the syndicate wanted him dead. Was that the truth? She wasn't sure, if only because he came clean that he agreed to sell her out to them in an effort to buy time to get out of the city and thus save himself. Would he do so again? Of course, he would. Worse, if she was in his situation, she'd do the same thing, which complicated things. To their core, survival was at the root of who they were. It's all they had. To keep going, to stay alive, they had to put themselves first. How could she judge him for any of this when she likely would have done the same thing in that situation?

Frustrated with her, he leaned back in his seat and crossed his legs, removing himself from any further conversation. She felt conflicted. Was she making a mistake by not seeking his help? She wasn't sure, but what she did know is that the man seated in front of her was someone she could never trust the way she trusted Spocatti.

CHAPTER
TWENTY-FIVE

Time passed and it passed slowly. How long had she been here now? A day? More than a day? Probably more than a day, though it felt like three. Maybe longer, but she knew that wasn't true. They'd yet to feed her, though when she asked, they did allow her to use the bathroom, which was just across from her, and they did allow her to use the water fountain next to the restroom when she said she was thirsty.

Each time they allowed her freedom beyond the chair, they gave her opportunities they couldn't understand. They had dismissed her because of her age. They had no idea what she had seen in her life, what she had been through or how she had survived as long as she had in a world that seemed determined to conspire against her.

Chloe Philips, brought to St. Vincent's when she was eight, looked at things differently than most because she had a worldview that was different from most. She looked for the advantage, whatever might give her the edge should she need it, which often was the case on the streets, especially when you were as relentlessly bullied as she was.

In her case, she was bullied because everyone at her school considered her the freak no one wanted, the girl who had failed to be adopted, unlike her sister, Mia, who found a family in a matter of months. Not so for Chloe. For eight years, she had been passed over time and again by dozens of families seeking a child of their own, and as such, she was considered broken. Worthless. At school, she was reminded of that daily.

The only person who alleviated the shame and burden that came from all of this was Carmen, whom she loved and who was the only reason she hoped to survive now. What they said about her being an assassin was a lie. She decided she didn't believe it. She wanted her relationship to continue with Carmen, who had been nothing but good to her, so she decided she would make an effort for that to happen.

Within reason.

Here, in this museum of grossly expensive cars, of which there had to be sixty or more, all gleaming under a single spotlight strategically placed above them, she'd seen a few opportunities on her way to the bathroom and to the water fountain that gave her a trace of hope that she might be able to shake things up in her favor.

Keeping her face a stoic mask, she had started to process those opportunities in ways that might help her to escape should a window open and present a wedge of freedom to her. Not that she expected that to happen. In her life, windows didn't open. Things always seemed sealed shut.

Knowing that, she knew herself well enough to know that she wouldn't be kept like an animal forever, regardless of how much she cared for Carmen and wanted to see her again. She wasn't afraid of taking risks—or facing her own death, for that matter, which she thought would have happened years ago when her mother brought home that idiot who struck her with a frying pan and did other unspeakable things to her and her sister.

But she also knew how to be calculating when it made sense to do so. As it did now.

The warehouse in which they kept her held two possibilities for a way out. She'd seen the exit, which was to her right and probably twenty yards away. Was it locked? Of course it was, but that didn't mean under the right circumstances it couldn't become unlocked.

Still, accomplishing that would be difficult, if not impossible, which is why she liked her other choice better, the one that involved using her mouth, the box she noticed on an earlier trip to the bathroom and how each of those, coupled with the Russian's precious sports car collection, could be used to get her the hell out of here.

When they first arrived, the Russian employed two armed men to guard her. But as the hours passed and the men grew restless, they suggested in front of her that they should take turns watching her. They asked the Russian if this was acceptable, he agreed to it, and now one of the guards was resting somewhere in the rear of the warehouse. From where she sat, she had no idea where he was because the space was too deep. She couldn't see him, which likely would become an issue.

The man at her right had been with her for several hours. A rifle was slung over his left shoulder. He held a gun in his right hand, which was perhaps a foot away from her. Maybe less. As for the Russian, he was working his phone, calling people, pacing between his cars, looking agitated, while cooking up a plan she supposed had to do with her.

She reached up her cuffed hands to brush her hair out of her face. The guard standing beside her looked down, then looked away. He was a brute—tall and built, his broad chest straining against his black T-shirt—but he was starting to look fatigued to her, which was good so long as he didn't decide it was time to wake his buddy and tell him that it was his turn to watch her. If that happened, she'd have someone refreshed standing beside her. More alert. She decided that if she was going to do this, she needed to act soon, because she feared if she didn't, things would be more difficult for her.

What the man standing beside her didn't know is that each time she lifted her hands to her face or bent down to scratch an itch that didn't exist on her ankle or calf is that she was seeing how much range of motion she had with her hands cuffed in front of her.

It wasn't ideal—she couldn't reach her back, for instance—but she expected that and it wasn't much of an issue when it came to pulling off what she had in mind.

She looked over at the Russian, who paced in front of his fancy cars while talking on his phone some thirty feet away to her right. Did he have a gun? She wasn't sure. When he was near her earlier, she couldn't see any signs of one, but that didn't mean he didn't have one concealed beneath the jacket he wore.

She listened to his conversation and wondered who was on the other line. He was giving directions to the warehouse and for the first time, she knew where she was. She was in Hell's Kitchen on West Forty-Sixth Street, right off Eleventh Avenue near the Hudson.

The irony that she was in Hell wasn't lost on her.

"It's better that we do it here," she heard him say. "Here makes sense. The girl's here. Also, Carmen doesn't know I own this space. It will seem like neutral ground to her. You need to bring her here."

There was a silence while he listened. "That's fine," he said. "How soon before you can have her here?" Silence. "I'll see you both in an hour. I like your plan, Vincent, but you need to be mindful of the cars. My collection is here. When you arrive, you'll see cars everywhere and I don't want anything to happen to them. Is that clear? Nothing can happen to them. When you take them down, I want it to be quick and clean, with nothing happening to my cars. That's right. They're that expensive. And fuck you on whether I have them insured."

He severed the connection, pulled out a pack of cigarettes from his inside jacket pocket, and it was then that Chloe saw the holster and his gun. He lit one of the cigarettes, exhaled over his head in a plume of billowing blue smoke that crowned one of the lights, and took to his phone again. He was so deep in thought as he tapped out numbers that she knew if she didn't act now, she'd miss her moment.

It all came down to timing. Everything did in life. She learned that when she left her mother, which probably saved her life. Could she beat death twice?

Time to find out.

Resolved to go forward, her heart quickened in her chest. Adrenaline cut through her like spears, pricking every part of her until she felt fully alive in the face of death. She took a breath, thought it through, memorized the space again, and then acted.

She reached down as if to scratch her ankle, glanced to her right, saw the guard's bare arm holding the gun at his side—and then she made her move as quickly and as viciously as possible.

In a flash, Chloe Philips's teeth were buried in the man's forearm. With everything she had in her, she sank her teeth in deep, she met bone, she carved through the thick muscle and tore off a piece of his forearm. She spat it out on the floor, felt blood gush into her mouth and willed herself not to get sick from the sheer amount she swallowed and which now covered her. Stunned by the act, the man dropped his gun, which Chloe picked up just as he was about to kick it across the floor.

Instead, his foot connected with her left shoulder, which seemed to crumble due to the sheer momentum behind the kick, but not before she had the gun held clumsily in her hands and stuck out in front of her. He shouted out in rage and in pain, and then for help, but Chloe Philips, born to the streets and bullied for much of her sad, rotten life, knew she had him even before she aimed shakily at his head and put a bullet through his throat.

Surprise filled his eyes. He looked genuinely shocked when he fell to his knees, which cracked from the force of the fall. Blood spurted onto the concrete floor. He covered the wound with his hand, but since Chloe hit his carotid artery, there was no saving him or stopping the rush of blood that pulsed through his fingers now.

She was aware of movement on either side of her. Katzev and the other guard. Time was of the essence even though time had seemed to stop.

For the moment, there was one thing left to do.

In spite of the pain in her shoulder, Chloe rolled onto her stomach and looked at the metal box attached to the wall at the far right of the water fountain. It was the breaker box. Had to be, given all the thick wires sinking into it and snaking out of it. Just as Katzev lifted his gun at her, Chloe took aim at the box, put a bullet through it, and winced as sparks flew into the room.

Instantly, the warehouse was plunged into a darkness so thick and black, she couldn't see anything but her own memory of the space.

She scrambled to her feet, held the gun out in front of her and moved blindly behind one of Katzev's cars. The pain roared in her dislocated left shoulder. She bumped against the car and winced. Would the alarm go off? It didn't. She hid behind the car. She listened and she waited.

In spite of the dark, he'd come for her now. So would his guard.

But she had a plan for that, too.

CHAPTER
TWENTY-SIX

"Max," Babe said after the knock came at the door it. "That will be Vincent. You know what he looks like. Check the security monitor and make certain it's him before you open the door. He'll want to be off the street quickly, so let him in as soon as possible and bring him to us."

Max nodded and left the room.

Babe looked over at Carmen with concern on her face. "I feel as if you need us," she said as Carmen and Jake stood. "I don't think we've done enough. I don't like this idea of you going in alone with Vincent—and not because of Vincent. But because Katzev is duplicitous. We both know it's not going to be just him and another guard wherever you're meeting him. He's going to have a team waiting for you. This is a setup. Doesn't that concern you? I know you've thought this through."

"Of course, I have," Carmen said. "But what can I do? Gelling is dead. Gone with him are the names of the syndicate members he was trying to compile for me."

"Have you thought of calling Gelling's assistant, Frank? You know, that enormous man with the watch that covers his bum eye? He's been with Gelling for years. He might know something."

Carmen looked defeated. "When I used the restroom a moment ago? I called Frank. He says he has no knowledge of any list."

"That's just bullshit," Babe said. "That man knows everything about Gelling. He wiped the man's ass, for God's sake. I don't believe it for a minute."

"Neither do I. But without his help and without that information, I have nothing to blackmail Katzev with. He has the upper hand with Chloe. He knows I'll do anything to keep her safe. Like it or not, as neutral as all this is supposed to be, he's running the show."

"But you have Liam," Babe said. "You have Katzev's family right in the palm of your hand. Certainly, that's something. One call to Liam and their lives are on the line. That's got to trouble Katzev. Liam could kill the man's mother, for God's sake."

"I don't think he cares for any of them, Babe."

"Why?"

"Because they aren't the syndicate, which is his world. It's what he built with Jean-Georges and what paid off so well for them. You saw Liam's video. As rich as Katzev is, his family is struggling. His mother was begging for help. The house behind them was in need of repair. There wasn't a single one of them who looked affluent." She held up a finger. "But wouldn't they if Katzev was helping them? For whatever reason, he's not. I think he made a conscious decision to distance himself from them. When it comes to saving the one thing that's made him the wealthy man he is today, they don't mean a damn thing to him. They come last."

At that moment, Spocatti was ushered into the room. Carmen looked over at him and couldn't help feeling relief. He was dressed in a black T-shirt, black jeans, and a black jacket to hide whatever he was carrying. He wore black shoes with the sort of soles that could dig into pavement or concrete or hardwood, while giving him plenty of traction to run should he need to.

She hadn't seen him in a while, but age hadn't touched him. He still had the masculine face of a boxer, which he used to be in his youth, and the dark brown eyes she remembered so well because they seemed to reflect the darkness of everything he knew and had created during his lifetime. His full head of dark hair gleamed with whatever product he had in it. He was fit and tanned from his time in Capri, and, seeing him now, she thought he was a force. The presence he brought into the room was something few possessed, but which he came by naturally.

He nodded at her.

Before she could return the gesture, Babe said, "Vincent." She walked over and moved aside his extended hand so she could give him a fleeting embrace, during which time she kissed him on each cheek before parting from him. There was something about the way she leaned into him with her right foot raised behind her that told Carmen everything she needed to know about their relationship. Here the young assassin with whom she said she once had an affair. Here was the man who opened her eyes to the dangerous life she had led for two decades.

"How was your trip?" she asked.

"Busy."

"And Capri?"

"Busier."

"You look well."

"We'll see how I look tomorrow morning." He looked across the room at Jake, who was standing in front of one of the red chairs. "Jake," he said.

"Vincent."

"In some trouble yourself, I hear."

"I'd like to join you tonight," he said. "I'd like to help. Katzev also came after me. Carmen can take him out, but I want him to see him die."

"Can't. It's just me and Carmen. That's the promise I made to get to Chloe. But I appreciate the offer."

"It's not just going to be the two of you," Babe said.

"I'm aware of that."

"Then let him help. He has very good reasons for wanting to see Katzev dead."

"It's not going to happen, Babe. Besides, Carmen and I can handle Katzev and the boys. We'll get Chloe out and then deal with the rest of them."

"Who's going to collect Chloe?" Jake asked.

"She'll be told to run."

"If that's the case, wherever you're meeting them, I can be parked along the street and get her when I see her."

"But you won't stay in your car, Jake," Spocatti said. "We both know that. We both know you want your own revenge against Katzev and the syndicate for trying to knock you off. I get it. They came after you. They nearly killed you. But this is Carmen's night. If anyone puts a bullet through Katzev's face, it's her."

"I won't interfere. I just want to watch."

"You're too hot right now. I don't believe that."

"Why are you shutting me out?"

"I'm not shutting you out. I made a deal with Katzev. He agreed to see me and Carmen—period. This is not personal, so stop behaving as if it is." He looked at Carmen. "When we tell Chloe to run, do you think she'll be all right? On the streets, I mean. Will she be safe?"

"She's tougher than she should be at her age, but nothing will help her if he has men surrounding the place, which is a possibility." She looked over at Jake.

"Maybe we need to rethink this. What he's proposing isn't a bad idea."

"It's just us, Carmen."

She felt another sting of worry for Chloe. She was becoming increasingly uncomfortable with how this was unfolding. She tried again. "I think we should reconsider."

But Spocatti held firm. "I don't. Here's why I'm fine with it being just us. Katzev has been told that if anything happens to either of us—or to Chloe—that I've contacted friends who will track him down and take him out at once. These people are loyal to me. I've saved their lives. They'll do it without hesitation. I've told Katzev that. I think we'll be fine, but I agree. We need to be prepared if he does something stupid."

"Prepared how?"

"We need to be alert."

"That's all?"

He didn't answer.

"Where are we meeting them?"

He looked at Babe and Jake. "No offense to you two, but I need to tell her in private." He checked his watch. "Get your gear. Babe has everything you need in her basement. We leave in ten."

"You two go to the basement," Babe said to Carmen and Spocatti. She wasn't used to being shut out so harshly and she looked angry because of it. "Take what you need. I'm having a drink."

* * *

When Carmen and Spocatti left eight minutes later, loaded with concealed guns and pockets full of ammunition, they thanked their hostess, who stood to walk them to the door, but they said nothing to Jake, who sat in one of the red chairs, pointedly looking away from them. He was furious with them. It was clear. It wasn't until Spocatti and Carmen left that Babe immediately swept back into the parlor in a hurry.

"That girl is headed straight into danger," she said. "Where are you parked?"

"Just down the street."

"Perfect. Max!" she called. "Grab my running shoes. Quickly."

She started to kick off her shoes, but kept her eyes on his. "They're getting a cab," she said. "We have moments before we lose them. I'm assuming you have useful things in your car? Things that will be meaningful if pointed at someone's face?"

"I have a trunk filled with just that."

Max entered the room with her running shoes, which she stepped into.

"I don't say this lightly, but I don't agree with Vincent. I don't know why he's being so unreasonable. Somebody has to be there to grab that girl when she's released from the building. Otherwise, I don't know what will happen to her. And what's the point of all of this if somebody doesn't help her?"

"We get the girl," he said. "They get Katzev. I just want to be there when it happens. I want to know that he's dead."

"Then let's go while there's still time to follow them. Come on. We might have already lost them."

CHAPTER
TWENTY-SEVEN

In the darkness she created, Chloe Philips waited.

She could hear footsteps, some so close, she began to sweat along her brow and down the small of her back. They were searching for her. Eventually, they'd find her. Then what? Shoot them? If her life was on the line, she'd have no choice.

"Chloe," the Russian said. "Come out. Now."

He was off to her right. Close enough that she started to tremble. Her dislocated shoulder was becoming too much for her to bear, but she forced herself to push through it. She was crouched low behind one of his ridiculous sports cars and held the gun tightly in front of her in her cuffed hands. She anticipated him to make a move at any moment. Could he hear her breathing?

She could hear him breathing...

"Don't be stupid, Chloe. Why die when you have every chance to live? Carmen is on her way to settle things for you. You still have hope if you decide to reveal yourself to us and behave. Otherwise, I'll make a call and ask the men waiting outside to come in and sweep this place for you. It won't be pleasant."

Earlier, she had crept away from the center of the warehouse, where the bathroom and water fountain were, knowing that they'd look for her there first, which they had.

Now, she was nearly at the warehouse entrance. She'd run for it, but it would be fruitless. There was no way that warehouse door was unlocked. She'd need to wait it out for Carmen, if she was indeed coming, which once again raised the question about why Carmen was involved in this—whatever *this* was. It didn't make sense to her.

"It's so dark in here," the Russian said. "Pitch black. Can't see shit, which was her point, I suppose. But it doesn't have to be that way, does it, Michael? We are, after all, surrounded by dozens of cars that have something she didn't think of. You know, things like headlights."

He stopped walking. There was a swishing sound, as if he suddenly turned around, perhaps because he thought he'd heard her, but then a moment passed and he continued to walk away from her again. "Michael," he said, "why don't you start turning on headlights and we'll get this over with before Carmen and Spocatti arrive?"

To her far right, all the way to the rear of the warehouse, where the guard called Michael must have been resting earlier, she heard a car door swing open. Within an instant, headlights flashed and flooded that end of the warehouse with a blazing, neon-blue light that cut through the gloom.

"Turn on all of them," the Russian said. "Find out where she's hiding, but be careful. She still has the gun."

She heard footsteps walk across the space to the car directly opposite the one whose headlights were shining. A door opened, there was the sound of a click, and more light beamed into the room.

Now, even from where she was crouched low, she could see the faint outline of things she hadn't been able to see before, including the Russian, whose gun was poised in front of him while he looked around the room for her. What a fool she had been. She'd never thought about the headlights. It wouldn't be long before they found her.

Another door opened. More light cut into the room. She took a breath and knew she had no choice. Taking out the guard and the breaker box was only the first part of her plan. Now, for the second part.

Before they could fully see her, Chloe Philips stood, aimed her gun at the hood of one of the cars glimmering in the light, and fired a bullet into it.

Sirens went off. The jolt of the gun almost caused her to blackout due to the pain in her drooping shoulder. She staggered back against a wall and braced her shoulder against it for support. She wanted to cry out in pain, but didn't.

"What the fuck are you doing?" the Russian shouted above the car's alarm. She heard real fear in his voice. Did he love his cars that much? Or was it the alarm that worried him? "Do it again and I'll kill you myself."

She turned to another car, aimed at it, and shot, destroying the hood and likely a good deal of the engine, which would kill the car's value and be difficult to repair.

"You want more?" she said, above the screams of the two alarms.

"She's at the front," she heard the Russian say. "Get her."

She couldn't hear them moving given the sound of the alarms, but she was sure one of them was rushing in her direction.

Go for it. All of it. Show them that you're serious.

Chloe sank a bullet into the hood of another car, but this time she missed and smashed out the car's front window, which caused its alarm to go off. She steadied her aim as best she could, shot again and this time struck gold. She hit the hood, a small fire erupted beneath it, and it started to smoke and bake from the heat. If she was thinking it, they were thinking it. If they didn't act fast, the car would explode.

"Keep the fuck away from me!" she shouted. "Come closer and I'll ruin all of your precious cars!"

"Quick," she heard the Russian say. "The fire extinguisher. Put out the fire before the sprinklers go off. You know what will happen if they do."

Chloe also knew what would happen. If the sprinkler system went off, the fire department would be notified. St. Vincent's had a sprinkler system. They also had an evacuation plan. She and the others were told what to do and where to meet outside should the fire alarm and the sprinkler system go off. They were told that the fire department and the police would automatically be alerted if either went off. The idea of the sprinklers going off here and the ramifications for these men if they did gave her an unexpected rush of power.

But her power didn't rest just there. There was something to be said for those shrieking alarms.

How many cars did she have to shoot before the alarms created such a commotion that someone called the police, if only to stop the noise, assuming it was bothering someone? From the address she heard earlier, she knew she wasn't in a residential neighborhood. Also against her is that she didn't know what time it was. Was is light out? Were there any businesses open? She didn't know. And what about the people driving by on the street? Could they hear the alarms? If they could, would someone make a call?

She knew better than that.

Still, the alarms were something. They were better than nothing. They were a possible way out, just like the sprinkler system was should it go off and alert the fire and police departments. She had to use whatever tools she had to get out of here and those alarms could be key.

She looked around the space, her shoulder aching. The sound from three cars already was at a piercing level, but they were at the rear of the warehouse, away from the two large doors at her left, which faced the street. Did it make a difference that the cars she shot were so far away from those doors? She squinted through the dim light and looked at the car closest to the doors. She wondered. She thought it through.

She didn't know how many bullets she had left, but she assumed she had some left. She knew nothing about guns, but she did know that what she held in her hand looked sophisticated. Like something she'd see in an action movie. She needed to use her ammunition sparingly, but this might be worth it.

She braced her shoulder against the concrete wall she was leaning against, aimed and shot the hood of the car across from her. Again she missed and hit the window, but it was enough to set off the alarm, which was so much louder here, it gave her hope.

The Russian shouted something. She could see them using the fire extinguisher to put out the fire beneath the hood, which now was lifted high and being gassed by the other guard, Michael. She looked up at the ceiling and wondered why the sprinklers hadn't gone off. There wasn't a great deal of smoke, but there certainly was enough to set them off. So, why hadn't they gone off? The warehouse was old. Were the systems old?

Did the sprinklers even work?

CHAPTER
TWENTY-EIGHT

In the cab they snagged on Park, they drove across Central Park, down to West Forty-Seventh Street, stopped for a traffic light, and turned left onto Eleventh Avenue.

It was dark. Given their proximity to the Hudson, the air here was cooler, but it also was humid. Worse, it was soured by a day's worth of exhaust from the shipping trucks that clogged the streets during the daytime, the smell of oil from the barges crowding the river and the filth that was everywhere.

On West Forty-Sixth, they saw the warehouse ahead of them and to their left, heard the sirens screaming from inside the building, and drove past as

Carmen lifted a hand to her face out of concern for Chloe.

Whatever was happening inside was either just beginning or, knowing Katzev, who was quick to act, might already be over. Not knowing unnerved Carmen so much that she did what she always did when she was under great pressure. She shut down her emotions and became focused on the task at hand.

Spocatti told the driver to circle around again, but this time to let them off at Eleventh Avenue. Each wanted to carefully scope the area before they approached the warehouse.

"Why the sirens?" she asked.

"No idea."

"Obviously, something happened. The sirens will draw attention to them. Somebody might have called the police."

"If we were on Eighth or Ninth, where people live, I'd agree. But down here? It's different. Industrial. Because of the crime, no one is on the streets. There's a chance no one has called the police."

"And if they have?"

He shrugged. "Then we're fucked." He let a silence pass. "You know we were followed?"

"I do."

"Babe is with him. That's unprecedented."

"We can't control them," Carmen said. "If they want to park and grab Chloe if we manage to free her, fine. And frankly, even though we disagree on this, if they can, they'll keep her safe, which is a relief to me. If they involve themselves otherwise, we'll deal with them then."

Spocatti didn't answer. He looked over his shoulder as Jake's car, some two hundred yards back, slid into a spot that wasn't a parking space. A hydrant was there. They were perhaps eight buildings up from the warehouse with a clear view of the two large garage doors that faced it.

Carmen's cell phone buzzed in her pants pocket. She removed it, stared at the message for a moment, committed it to memory, and then, acting on instinct because she didn't want to share it with Spocatti, who was acting unusual for reasons she didn't understand, set things into motion with a few quick clicks.

"What was that?" he asked.

"That was private," she said. She regretted the edge in her voice—he was, after all, here to help her—and said, "Sorry. I'm just tense. It was an offer for a new job."

"From the syndicate?"

She was in no mood to joke. She didn't answer.

He put his hand on her knee, a kind gesture that also was unlike him. "It'll be all right, Carmen. Katzev won't take my threat lightly. We just need to get in there in case someone does call the police."

"If they haven't already."

"Understood."

The driver pulled to the curb.

"With those sirens going off, we don't know what we're walking into."

"When do we ever know?" He opened his door and gave the driver five hundred dollars. "That's for your discretion," he said.

The man looked at the money and casually pocketed it. "Not sure what you're talking about, man, but thanks."

Spocatti stepped out and looked at Carmen. He was about to say that they needed to get inside when, for the first time, he noticed them. "You're wearing those?" he asked.

"I always wear these, just not on planes."

"Do they still work?"

She showed him.

"Rosa Klebb would be proud, though she'd miss the knitting needles. How long does it take?"

"Twelve seconds."

"Ugly way to die."

"He shouldn't have snatched my girl."

His eyes flicked up to meet hers. "You plan on using them?"

"If I have the chance."

"And you plan to sacrifice yourself for Chloe? You really mean to do this?"

"If it comes to that, I will. But have you forgotten? You threatened Katzev. A moment ago, when you told Jake that he wouldn't be joining us, you essentially said your threat would be enough to put the fear of God in Katzev if anything happens to us. Beyond that, I have Liam in Aberdeen and he will slaughter Katzev's family with a press of a button on my cell. I plan on using that against, Katzev. We'll see how loyal he is to his mother, who will die first.

I'm not going out without a fight, Vincent. So, let's get this over with."

CHAPTER
TWENTY-NINE

"I see them," Jake said. "They're coming around the corner. Spocatti has his cell in his hand. Now at his ear."

Babe craned her head so it was closer to the passenger-side window. The street was dim but with some effort, she could see them. "He must be calling Katzev."

"Likely."

"To get inside."

"Obviously."

"I'm concerned about the alarm."

"Everyone should be."

"What do you think happened?"

He shrugged. "I've been forced out of the loop on this. No idea. I hope they can handle it on their own."

The clipped tone of Jake's voice made Babe McAdoo turn to look at him. As dim as it was in the car, she could see him watching Carmen and Spocatti intently. Though his features were neutral, she sensed anger brimming beneath the surface. In her life, she'd dealt with too many men and women in this profession to take that anger lightly. He felt slighted. Could he contain those feelings? If not, what then? She chose her words carefully. "I'm sorry you feel that way," she said.

"You don't know what I feel, Babe."

She offered nothing more. Best to back off, though tension in the car was high. She turned to the window and noticed that Spocatti and Carmen were standing outside one of the garage doors. Spocatti was on his cell, talking. Carmen was a step behind him, looking up and down the street, and also up at the windows of the buildings surrounding them. A sniper could be in one of them. Her hands were buried in her jacket pockets, gripping her Glocks should she need them.

When the shrill of the alarm began to lessen, Babe rolled down her window an inch and listened. Earlier, she assumed it was just one alarm going off. Instead, it was several alarms, which now were being turned off one by one.

"Do you hear that?" Babe asked. "I thought it was just the alarm for the warehouse. But listen. A number of alarms are going off. Or were going off. Like car alarms. He must have cars in there."

When he replied, it was as if he was speaking to a child. "That's right, Babe. They were car alarms. If it had been an alarm for the warehouse, knowing Katzev, it would have been silent and gone straight to the syndicate, which would have deployed a small army comprised of those assassins not considered end-of-cycle. I don't know what set off the alarms or what's happening in there now, but Katzev obviously found his keys and is shutting them down now."

He didn't even try to conceal the chill in his voice. She knew he was angry that he wasn't asked to join Carmen and Vincent since he himself had been targeted by the syndicate, so she sat there, watching the warehouse, until the final alarm was silenced. After a moment, one of the garage doors lifted and they were allowed inside an entrance that was in pitch darkness. She tried to see if anyone was there to greet them, but it was too dark to see. The garage door slid shut behind them and they were gone.

"They're in there now," she said, more to herself than to him. She was worried for them.

"So, they are."

"Why was it so dark? What do you think will happen?"

"Who knows?"

Given his tone, he might as well have said, "Who cares?" She decided to ignore it and stay on task. "So, we wait for Chloe."

"Babe," he said, as if he hadn't heard her. "Why do you suppose Spocatti didn't want me in there with them? We've worked together several times over the years. He knows I'm more than competent. He also knows the syndicate wants me dead. Why would he cheat me of having my moment to join Carmen in taking out Katzev?"

"Those are a lot of questions, Jake. And I'm not Vincent. I can't answer for him. But I know he supports you fully. He knows you've joined us in helping to bring down the syndicate."

"He's always been an arrogant son of a bitch," Jake said, ignoring her. "Comes in on his white horse and takes over. How did that happen?"

"It just happened."

"But how?"

"People respect Vincent. You know as well as I do that he's the best. Nobody is as good as he is."

"According to who? Where did he get that reputation?"

He was starting to make her anxious. "You know how good he is. Everyone does. He earned it."

"Who decided he earned it? Have I earned anything? Why do you put him on a pedestal like that?"

She turned to him. "Why are you doing this?"

"I'm just looking for answers."

"I'm giving you what I can, but I don't have all of them."

"Then, what good are you to me?"

Her right hand dropped to her side, where in her pocket was the gun he gave her earlier. But Babe McAdoo was too late. Jake pulled his gun on her and pointed it at her face. There was a silencer at the end of it. He pressed the trigger just slightly and a tiny red laser beam pierced the narrow distance between them. It found its place in the center of her forehead. She stared openly at him in shock.

"You're in my way," he said.

"I'm not—"

"You should be supporting me."

"I do support you."

"I should be in there. They sent two men to kill me. Katzev sent them. One probably would have killed me if he wasn't run over by a truck. Why should I be denied the right to see him die? Why shouldn't I have a hand in his death? Why am I considered so inferior that I can't be part of this? That wasn't the deal. I came in to be part of this. I never expected to be some fucking bystander."

"You're taking this too personally."

"No, I'm not."

Regardless of her quickening heart, she managed to keep her voice steady. "Here's what's personal," she said. "You have a gun held to my face. A laser shining on my forehead. That's as personal as it gets. Would you please put that away? I'm not against you, Jake. I told you. I support you."

"How do I know that? You know what I look like, Babe. On a whim, if you wanted to, you could identify me and turn me in."

At that moment, she realized how little she knew about him since she brought him in to surprise Carmen and assist her. During their time together, he'd given away practically nothing about himself, with the exception that Katzev had used his men to try and kill him. She'd been so caught up in trying to help Carmen that she hadn't paid much attention to him or to his behavior.

"I know what many of you look like," she said. "I opened my home to you and offered you a safe haven from Katzev and the syndicate. I agreed with you that Spocatti shut you out of this, which is why we're here now. We're doing something. We're waiting for Chloe. We're going to save her. I've been trying to help all of you."

"You sound desperate, Babe."

"You haven't lowered the gun. I have good reason."

"I think I'll take care of this myself. Starting with Spocatti. I never liked him. It's time he knows that he's not King Shit around here."

Her eyes filled with sorrow. She knew what was coming and she knew well enough that she was powerless to stop it.

"Jake," she said.

"Shut up, Babe."

"I would never betray you."

"I don't know you. I don't believe you."

"I'm here for you," she said. "Please rethink this. I've devoted twenty years of my life to helping your people."

"*My* people. What does that mean? That I'm not a McAdoo? That I'm not one of *your* people?"

"That's not what I meant at all."

"I think it is what you meant."

"Why are you doing this?"

"Survival."

Before she could lift her hands to protect herself, he fired two shots into her face, her head slammed against the passenger-side window in a bloody yellow smear, and Babe McAdoo of the famed McAdoo family, which was long known and celebrated for its variety of seasonings, particularly during the holiday season when everyone seemed to use them, mostly for turkey or roasted chicken, which were improved by them, was dead.

CHAPTER THIRTY

Carmen and Vincent had their guns drawn and poised in front of them the moment they saw that the warehouse was in darkness.

The door was opened manually. Whoever opened and closed it hurried away. The room smelled of smoke and something else Carmen couldn't define. A fire extinguisher? Made sense, only the reason it had been used was unknown. She scanned the darkness for Chloe—for anyone—but she couldn't see anything.

"We've been set up," she said to Spocatti. "They could be wearing goggles. Infrared."

"Let me deal with this." He took a step forward. "Turn on the lights, Katzev. Don't fuck with me. You'll lose. Turn them on now."

At the rear of the room came a flicking sound followed by a tiny flame igniting in the gloom. Carmen squinted and could see the faint outline of Katzev's face. He held the lighter out in front of him, which cast unflattering shadows upon his face. She'd never seen him before, but this is how she'd come to view him in her mind. With the shadows curling around his jaw and beneath his eyes, he looked demonic to her. Evil.

"Settle down," he said. "We don't have lights because Carmen's girl shot the breaker box after killing one of my men. Nothing I can do about it. You're lucky there's a manual override on that garage door so we could let you inside."

"You're telling me you have no emergency lighting in this joint? Bullshit," Spocatti said. "I don't believe it."

"Believe it. The building is old, Vincent. When she set fire to one of my cars, even the sprinkler system didn't work. Otherwise, we'd be doused and the fire and police departments would be here."

Carmen processed the information quickly. Somehow, Chloe got hold of a gun. She killed one of Katzev's men. Probably shot several cars, which would explain the sirens she heard earlier. One or more of the bullets must've created a fire. For a period of time, she had them all scrambling while she likely found a place to hide. *Smart girl*, she thought. *Reckless, but smart. Now, where are you?*

"Where is Chloe?" Spocatti asked.

"No idea," Katzev said. He stepped forward and as he did, Carmen saw in the aura of light around him that a man with a rifle was leaning over the hood of one of the cars. The rifle was braced against his shoulder and pointed at them. "The murdering little bitch disappeared. She's in here, somewhere. And don't worry about the lack of light. I've got that covered. It's coming."

"With more of your men?" Carmen asked.

"That's how the light is getting here, Carmen."

"Why do I feel that's awfully convenient, Iver?"

He paused at the mention of his real name. She could almost sense him bristling at the sound of it. That she'd even dare to use it in his presence and in front of his men. "Think what you want," he said. "But it's your girl who created this. Now, it's up to me to fix it. Otherwise, we're all in the dark."

"Which is how I feel right now," she said to Spocatti in a low voice.

"Not that the lighting situation is difficult to fix," Katzev said, flicking off the cigarette lighter. "Turn on the lights."

In rapid succession, headlights from every car that hadn't been damaged by Chloe started to turn on in such a way that they raced from where Spocatti and Carmen stood down to the very end of the warehouse, where Katzev stood.

For a moment, Carmen couldn't see anything—the headlights were on high, which in the wake of the absolute darkness she was just in, blinded her. She held up her hand to shield her eyes, and noticed that Spocatti simply stood there, squinting into the light as he stared forward.

"What happened to just him and another guard?" she said to him. "We're surrounded."

Car doors opened and slammed shut. Footsteps sounded on concrete. Armed men walked around to the front of each car in which they were sitting, guns and rifles now trained on her and Spocatti.

They were being ambushed. Why wasn't Spocatti saying anything? And where was Chloe? Beneath one of the cars? Probably. Hopefully somewhere more discrete. But regardless of where she was, in this light, Carmen feared it wouldn't be long before they found her and possibly killed her given that she killed one of their men.

"I know what you're thinking," Katzev said. "So many men. But when your Chloe broke our deal, I had no choice but to bring in all of my men to get things back on track."

"She knew nothing about our deal. How could she? If she killed one of your men, it was only because she was trying to save herself."

"Murdering one of my men will only end with her own death."

"No, it won't, for reasons you and I have already discussed," Spocatti said. "With the exception of you and your guard, which we agreed upon, I recommend that each of your men put down their guns, shove them under the car they're standing in front of and leave immediately. That was our agreement. Stick to it or there will be consequences."

But Katzev ignored him. He started to walk forward, galvanized by the fact that he had at least twenty of his own men guarding his back. "Do you know why you're here, Carmen?"

Due to the way the lights were shining, she could only see a shadowy figure walking toward her. She couldn't see Katzev's face. He still was an enigma to her.

"I assume it has to do with Alex?" she said. "Whom you murdered."

"And for good reason," Katzev said. "Alex was a rogue agent. He learned things about the syndicate that we're certain he shared with you, which is why you also were targeted for elimination."

"What things?"

"You tell me," he said.

"Alex shared nothing with me, Iver. I don't know what you're talking about. All I can tell you is what I've learned about you and the syndicate on my own. And it's a lot. If you don't stand down and let Chloe go free, the world will know everything about all of you."

"You don't intimidate me, Carmen."

"Then let me be clearer. I wonder if my knowledge of Hera Hallas would intimidate Ms. Hallas enough to suffocate your ties to the syndicate? Or Conrad Bates, who hates you? Or Marius Albert, who lives in Paris and feels the same way about you? Or any other member of the syndicate? I've done my homework, Iver, and I know who all of you are. This has nothing to do with Alex, who kept your secrets, even though he wrongfully died because you thought he was a rogue agent. I'm here to tell you that he took your secrets to his death. He died for nothing. You stole him away from me. So here I am, cashing in on my revenge, which I'll have—one way or another."

"You better back off, girl," Katzev said. But as tough as he made his fake Russian accent sound, a slight note of concern was wedded to it. Carmen heard it and seized upon it.

"What I've learned about you and the others has everything to do with me and my contacts. Or, should I say, one very special contact who died this evening, but whose employee reached out to me moments ago because he decided his employer would want me to have the information he worked so hard to compile for me. You'll never know who he is. But because of him, I have intelligence on you and every other member of the syndicate. Detailed intelligence, such as where you live, what you own, where you're invested, in which buildings you keep your corporate offices. Also, who you've targeted for death throughout the years. I've already set things in motion with my contact at the NYPD that if anything should happen to me tonight, the information I sent him earlier will be fully investigated, exposed, and made world news for all the wrongs you've done, which I think we'd both agree are plenty. Would you like me to run through the rest of the names, Iver? Yes? No? Because I can, just as I can stop your own family's deaths, which are about to happen in minutes, starting with your mother."

Spocatti turned to her in surprise. She could feel him looking at her. Reassessing her. Now he knew why she used her cell phone earlier. Now he knew, just as Katzev knew, that her information was true. Better yet, if he didn't know it before, there could be no question now that she was a force to be taken seriously.

"I need your guards to leave, Iver. And I mean to get the hell out of here and not to wait for us outside. I need for them to get in their cars and leave. When I'm certain they're gone, then you release Chloe, as agreed upon. Someone is outside to pick her up. Then Spocatti and I walk out of here. You will never contact me again. I will forget everything I know about you and the syndicate. That's my promise to you. As for Vincent, if you want to stay together, that's between you two. I really could give a shit. But if you ever come after me again, my contact is sitting on one million dollars, the key to which he'll only receive from an unknown source should the syndicate act upon me at any point going forward."

"And how will he know that it was us, Carmen? So many would like to see you dead. It could be us. It could be someone else who kills you. How will he know?"

She hadn't anticipated this question and thought quickly. "Iver, I know your hand. You show it so well. I always will know when I'm being followed by you. At that point, I'll alert my contact. Should anything happen to me, he'll know it's you, the keys and the money will be his—as will all the information on the syndicate, which should net him that fat promotion and publicity that have eluded him for years."

She lifted her arm to check her watch, the mere action of which caused several of the men surrounding her to lean into position with their guns and rifles. "Oh, please," she said to them. "Stand down. Did you not hear what I just said?"

Katzev lowered his hand and they relaxed.

"Your mother dies in twenty minutes unless my man hears from me. You've seen the video. You know he's there. None of this is bullshit, Iver. We're going to have a clean break from one another."

"But you've already said you're seeking revenge," Katzev said. "So, where is your revenge?"

"Are you blind? Have you not heard me? If you come after me at any point, the syndicate will be revealed and investigated at the highest levels. Including you. *That's* my revenge. It will continue when they bring all of you publicly to trial and then to prison. It will be a media circus. Your reputation will be destroyed. *That's* my revenge. But it doesn't end there. My revenge also is cheating you out of killing me. Should you be stupid enough to do so, face the law. Now, get your men out of here. Tell them to drive far and away. You need to move fast and take this seriously. We find Chloe and let her go. Then Vincent and I walk out. I don't know about him, but I'll be out of your life forever."

"About Spocatti," Katzev said. "He probably has that same contact at the NYPD. Or I'm sure he can find out who it is and offer him more money to just walk away from this and leave it alone when you die. When it comes to the man who you've hired to kill my family, I'm also fairly sure that Spocatti knows who it is and can make a phone call that will stop him. We'll pay him handsomely to do so."

He started to walk toward her. "You're so ignorant, Carmen. So assuming. Because what you don't know is this. Spocatti here? Your good friend, Spocatti. He has no conscience. It's what I love about him. It's why I will continue to work with him for as long as I'm alive. Without you or the love of your life, Alex, here to hire, it appears that he'll be terribly busy for many years."

He paused as Spocatti turned and drew his gun on her. She looked at him in bewilderment. She took a step back as the laser attached to his Glock 19 flashed out and wavered just beneath her right eye.

"What are you doing?" she said to him. Her voiced was laced with confusion. Was this a joke?

"What does it look like, Carmen?" Spocatti said. "I've been hired to kill you tonight. Nothing personal, so stop looking as if it is. It's what people like us do. Well, at least it's what people like me do. I take the job, I take the money, I follow through. I don't have your conscience. I kill children. I'm not interested in doing good. I'm only interested in me. Now turn around. Drop your gun. It's not ending the way you wanted it to."

CHAPTER
THIRTY-ONE

"Clear your men out," Spocatti said to Katzev when Carmen's gun hit the cement floor. "Nothing happens in front of this many people. It's not how I work, especially when all of your men are armed. If you plan on saving your mother, we're running out of time, Katzev. So, get them out."

"Why? They work for me. They're not going to say anything about this."

"You thought the same thing about Alex and Carmen before you murdered him and targeted her. Somebody in this room will be the next Alex and Carmen. Do you all hear that? I hope so. I hope you take it to heart, because it will happen. I also know that you know that, Katzev. If you want this done, get them out."

Facing death and deceit, Carmen tried to keep herself calm, but she couldn't. She had been betrayed by Spocatti. Used by him. She was angry and afraid, especially for Chloe, who had yet to reveal herself. "Why are you doing this, Vincent?" she said.

"Shut up, Carmen."

"Tell me why you're doing this."

"For the same reason you'd do it if you were offered twenty million dollars. You're nothing but a mark to me. If you thought differently about our relationship, you should have known better. There are no friends in this business. You of all people should know better. There's only the mark and the money."

"Bullshit. I'd never sell you out."

"Then you're an idiot." He pressed the barrel of his gun so hard against the back of her head that he scraped her scalp to the point that he drew blood. "I can make this quick and painless for you, or I can make it so you bleed out on the floor. Your choice. Run your mouth again and you'll get the latter." Then, to Katzev, he said, "I won't ask again. Get them out."

"One guard stays," Katzev said. "That's what we agreed upon. Me and another guard."

"Fine. The rest move. Thanks for your confidence in me, Katzev." Spocatti's voice reeked with sarcasm.

Katzev knew he had no choice and Carmen saw him wave his hand in the air. "Put your guns and rifles beneath your cars. When you leave, I expect you to get out of here. We'll finish this alone tonight."

All around her, she could hear the sounds of his men doing as they were told. Did she know any of them? Of course, she did. She'd probably worked with several of them, which deepened the betrayal.

What could she do to stall this? The answer was obvious, even though she knew Spocatti had the resources to crush it. Still, she had to try. "I told you that if anything happened to me, my contact will investigate the syndicate, Iver. Chloe and I walk out of here now. If we don't, the consequences will be swift. You'll regret it."

"He won't regret anything," Spocatti said. "Do you seriously believe I don't know who your contact is at the NYPD? Probably the same as mine. If it isn't, I can find out in ten minutes. Sorry it has to be this way, Carmen, but business is business. Katzev here has been generous. Looks like I'll be getting that villa in Capri sooner than I thought."

She was about to speak again, but this time he took his gun and whacked it so hard against the back of her head, the blow sent her to the gray edges of unconsciousness. She doubled over in pain. She felt faint and dizzy. The floor started to spin. Her knees buckled and she began to fall.

Spocatti stopped it from happening. He put his arm around her waist and lifted her up, holding her still until she was aware of one of the garage doors opening, men leaving, the door closing shut with a clatter and a bang, the sound of her own breathing, the world coming back into focus. She blinked hard. Her mind was a haze of fog and confusion. How had it come to this?

What was more painful to her is that she wouldn't have her revenge. She was being cheated out of taking out Katzev for what he'd done to Alex and to Chloe. The idea of failing as spectacularly as she had was like death itself. She'd let both down. She always knew she would die because of her work, but she never thought it would be at the hands of one of the few people she considered a friend.

Her head pounded. A wave of dizziness overcame her and she felt as if she was going to be sick. Her knees went again. Spocatti hoisted her up with a brutal jerk and she struggled to focus. Had to focus. Did she have a concussion? What a fool she'd been. How naive she'd been. Her thoughts turned to Chloe, who had listened to all this and who now knew things about her that she never should have known. Carmen knew they were going to kill her, but whatever part of her that believed she could still save Chloe came to the forefront. If she played her hand right, perhaps she could save Chloe, wherever she was.

"Iver," she said.

"What, Carmen?"

He was off to her right. She could hear him start to walk toward her. And then he stopped.

"Iver. Listen to me."

"You have her fully restrained?" he asked Spocatti.

"She's not going anywhere. Except maybe to hell in five minutes."

"What do you want, Carmen?"

"I want to see you before I die. I've never laid eyes you. I want to see what a monster looks like."

"You see one every day, Carmen. You see yourself. I'll never give you the pleasure of seeing me."

"The pleasure? Please. You don't have the balls to look me in the eye, Iver. It's that pussy Scot you have in you. If you were a real Russian, you'd come over here and probably slap me across the face. Or kill me yourself. But you don't have that big set of Russian balls you think you have, do you? From what I've heard, you actually have pebbles down there. And a little cock. It's why you hire people like me and Spocatti to do your dirty work. You've got a small one. I've heard all about it. I was told it was like a berry resting in a nest."

At the far end of the warehouse, the remaining guard stifled a laugh. It wasn't loud, but if she heard it, they all heard it and she could only imagine the fallout that person would endure because of it.

"Who said that?" Katzev said.

"I'll never give you the pleasure of knowing, Iver."

She heard him start to walk toward her. He was moving fast, determined to save face in front of his guard, who likely would mention this moment to the others. She knew he was carrying. She knew this was it for her. Loudly, to the room, she said, "Chloe, I'm sorry. I never meant for any of this to happen. Please forgive me."

Spocatti tightened his grip on her waist. He was strong and held her arms firmly at her sides. She struggled against him, tried to get to her phone to hit a button that would alert Liam to take out Katzev's family, but it was no use. She reached back to kick Spocatti, but he side-stepped her. "You can go to hell, Vincent."

"I'll let you check it out for me, first."

And then Iver Kester, whom she'd known for years only as the faceless, mysterious Katzev, stood in front of her. He was somewhere in his late forties, not yet fifty, which surprised her because in her mind's eye, she always expected him to be older than that, probably due to the power and money he had amassed.

His hair was dark and cut stylishly short. His eyes were blue, his complexion pale. He was fit. Probably just under six feet. He wore a black suit with a red tie and, if she was to be fair to him, she understood why Babe McAdoo was physically drawn to him all those years ago. In his youth, Iver Kester must have been something to behold.

"Iver," she said. "So, here you are. The last thing I'll see. What a vision you are."

He pulled back his hand and slapped her hard across the face. The force was so great and the slap so loud that Carmen rocked back against Spocatti, who held her firm. She used the distraction of the violence to press down and to the left on her right shoe, which silently released a blade that was two inches long. The blade was tainted with tetrodotoxin, the poison of the puffer fish, which essentially was a sodium channel blocker that paralyzed its victim's muscles while they remained fully conscious as they went through the death throes. With the poison in their system, the victim would quickly be rendered unable to breathe. Death from asphyxiation would ensue within twelve seconds.

She lifted her eyes to Katzev.

"You're going to kill me now. We both know that, so understand that what I'm going to tell you isn't a lie because there's no reason for me to lie. I'm finished. I'm off to check out hell for both of you and the rest of the syndicate. But here's what you need to know, Iver. Alex never betrayed you. Whatever you thought he knew about you or the syndicate died with him—if he knew anything at all. And I doubt that he did because he would have told me. The tragedy of his death comes down to why he really died—your own paranoia."

"There was a breach—" Katzev began.

"I don't give a damn what you thought there was. Alex knew nothing and you killed him. That's what matters to me. I came back to New York to have my revenge. And now look at me. Held back by a man I thought was my friend. Beaten. Facing death." She paused for a millisecond. "And still having my revenge."

In a flash, she kicked Iver Kester in the leg, buried the knife in the side of his calf, where the meat was, and left it there so the poison could leach into him.

Stunned by the act, Kester fell to the ground, his eyes already wide open and freezing into place as he stared up at her, struggling for breath, while she pulled out the blade.

Spocatti was swift. He released Carmen, swung his arm around, and shot the guard Kester left behind before he had time to process what was happening.

Carmen got down on one knee and put her mouth next to Kester's ear while his face started to turn pale blue from lack of oxygen. "You're dying, Iver," she whispered to him. "Soon, you'll leave your body and face Alex. I wonder what kind of meeting that will be?" She cocked her head at him while his eyes remained transfixed on hers. They were filled with tears. The beauty of the poison is that he could see her and hear everything she said.

She spit in his face. "I wonder if that meeting will be as pleasant as what's happening to you now?"

He started to make an odd gurgling noise. His tongue began to swell. She knew she had only seconds to act before she lost her chance. She reached into her pocket, removed her cell phone, and recorded the last few moments of Iver Kester's miserable life before it left him in one clotted, rattling last breath.

She clicked off her phone and lowered her head to her raised knee. She was exhausted and in pain. She breathed deeply and, looking down at Kester, whose face now was purple and without life, she realized how thankful she was that she could still breathe.

"What do you plan to do with that?" Spocatti said.

She planned to send the video to the syndicate with a warning that included all their information, but even though she knew now that Spocatti treated her roughly for show because he knew about her shoe, she didn't want to talk to him. She felt he took things too far. She messaged Liam in Aberdeen and told him to stand down. Now, all she wanted to do was to find Chloe. That was her focus.

She walked away from Spocatti and into the center of the warehouse, where she started to call out Chloe's name, telling her it was safe to come out, until she finally did. The girl had crawled beneath one of the cars. Since so many of the cars sat low to the ground, it was an effort for her to release herself from it, but because she was so slight, she managed to do so. When she was free, she stood shakily to her feet and Carmen noticed that her left shoulder was drooping. It was dislocated. She saw the pain on

Chloe's face as she ran toward Carmen with her gun still held in her hand.

"You're hurt," Carmen said.

Chloe slipped her right arm around Carmen's waist, put the side of her face against her chest, and they embraced. "It's just my shoulder," she said. "I'll be all right."

"I'm sorry," Carmen said. She held her face in her hands, saw the bruises and the split lip, and felt sickened by it. She looked down at Chloe's gun and took it away from her. "What did they do to you?"

"They hit me, but I can take it. It's not as if it hasn't happened before. I also killed a man, but he deserved it." She paused and looked Carmen in the eye. "They said you're an assassin. Is that true?"

Carmen wasn't sure how to proceed. For years, she had tried to be a positive influence on Chloe's life. But what was she to her now? An assassin. A murderer. She never wanted her to know that this life existed anywhere but in the movies, but now Chloe knew better. She had blood on her own hands. She may have acted in self-defense, but tonight she nevertheless had killed a man. Carmen knew that moment would be with her for the rest of her life.

"This all happened to you because of me, and I am sorry for all of it," she said. "We'll talk later about who I am. There are things about me that you need to know, but they can wait. Right now, we need to get out of here. I can fix your shoulder myself, but it will hurt."

"So, you're also a doctor?"

"I'm not a doctor, Chloe," Carmen said with a smile. "But I can fix your shoulder."

Spocatti was at the garage door, waiting for them.

"Ready?" he asked.

Carmen, angry with him, nodded.

He lifted the door and when he did, Jake, whose real name was Fred but who wisely went by Jake, was standing just outside the door, obviously distressed, hatred in his eyes, blood spattered on his face, his gun poised at Spocatti, which he quickly lifted to the man's head.

CHAPTER THIRTY-TWO

"Get back," Jake said. "Drop your guns."

Carmen dropped her gun and took a step back with Chloe, holding the girl behind her for protection while noting that the blade on her shoe was still extended. Her eyes flicked up to meet Jake's. Was there still poison on the blade? Certainly there was some, but how much did she need to kill him?

Spocatti started to move, but in an unexpected flash, his gun tipped upward and the bullet he put through Jake's jaw also nicked his brain and sent him into another world.

Carmen watched, unbelieving. It was so swift. Effortless. Jake fell to the floor and started to twitch and convulse as life left him. Vincent kicked his gun away and watched him for a moment before he took a step forward and leaned over him.

"Came to make a big scene, did you? Probably had it all planned, too. Sorry about that, buddy."

Blood bubbled up and started to seep out of the man's ears and nose. His brain was hemorrhaging. Carmen looked beyond him. They were exposed to the outside. Dozens of cars were behind them with their headlights on. If anyone saw them, they'd also see what was happening.

She quickly stepped forward, grabbed Jake by the back of his collar, and pulled him in so she could shut the garage door. It closed with a bang. Finished, she looked up at Chloe and saw the horror on her face.

"I wonder what your speech would have been, Fred," Spocatti said. "I'm sure you had one ready to deliver to me and to Carmen. Must suck that you can't say anything. Or, for that matter, that you'll never be saying anything again."

Jake, or Fred, whose last name was unknown to them, struggled in his last moments of life to look at Spocatti. It was an unfocused look. There was no longer hatred in his eyes. Instead, there was only the fight to stay alive, which he was losing.

Spocatti moved toward the garage door. He looked at Carmen, who was retracting the blade in her shoe. "I didn't come all the way from Capri for his bullshit," he said. "Let's go."

He opened the door and, before closing it, he turned back to look at the man who had come to kill them. "I'll make sure they put *Jake* on your tombstone, Fred." Then, to Carmen, he said, "I know I was rough. I apologize, but I had to make it look real if he was going to come around and face you. I knew you planned to use the shoe. You did well by Alex. And by Babe, whom I fear is dead given the blood on Jake's face. I think both would be proud of you right now."

Carmen reached into her pants pocket and removed her cell. Since she was alive, there was no need to wait. To her contact at the NYPD, she sent him everything she knew about the syndicate, which was enough to shut it down forever, and added a note that he should come here now if he wanted to receive the promotion both knew he wanted and deserved.

"We'll take our own cab," she said to Spocatti.

"Are we good?"

"We're in limbo."

"We should talk."

"Maybe in a year. I don't have time for you now."

Without another word, Carmen put her arm around Chloe's waist, pulled her close to her, and walked away, leaving Spocatti to close the garage door behind them and to escape into the night, just as he had done so many times before.

ABOUT THE AUTHOR

Christopher Smith is the #1 international best-selling author of "**Fifth Avenue**," its sequels "**Running of the Bulls**" and "**From Manhattan with Love**," as well as "**Bullied**," "**Revenge**," "**Witch**" and "**War**," all four of which deal with the subject of bullying. His newest thriller, "**A Rush to Violence**," is the first in a three-book series.

Prior to writing novels, for fourteen years, Smith was the film critic for a major newspaper in the Northeast. For eight years, he appeared weekly on NBC affiliates, and two years nationally on the E! network. He has written over 4,000 reviews and he has been named Best Critic for 2010 by the MPA. He has published two previous books in his Netflix "Queued" series, which are compilations of hundreds of his film reviews. He lives in Maine.

16867765R00171

Made in the USA
Charleston, SC
14 January 2013